Home

A Stranded Novel

By Theresa Shaver

Author's Note

Woo Hoo, what a ride! Four books in just over a year and the biggest surprise ever…most of you liked them lol! The reviews, suggestions and all the feedback, good and bad was so amazing and I truly believe it was what kept me going and made me a better writer. I just wanted to say thank you to everyone who supported me and asked for more. THANK YOU!

I love this book. It was a pleasure to write and I really think that it could be done in real life because of teenagers. Let me explain…How many parents in the world have yelled at their teenagers, "What were you thinking? You could have been hurt or killed!", when they've done crazy things? Teens still have that invincible feeling when it comes to their safety because they haven't been alive long enough to have it scared out of them. They do things and then think about them later. That's why I think they could rush in and save the day, because they just do it!

This book wraps up just about everything but I don't want to be done with these kids! So I'm asking for reviews and feedback on another book in the series. I have a great idea for another book where they have to survive a brutal Canadian winter and a sickness outbreak in their town. You guys let me know if you want more and I will write it! I've started a new series tentatively titled 'Endless Winter', about life during a nuclear winter that I'm really excited about. If I write another Stranded Novel, it will come after the first book in that series is published.

Now to the sappy stuff.

My Husband…Ten years and you still thrill my heart when you walk through the door. Thank you for every day.

My Kids…I'm sorry I'm working instead of playing Lego with you. Thank you for understanding and cheering me on. I love you both so much!

My Parents…For bragging about my work to complete strangers and being proud of me. YOU taught me what family means. I love you.

To My Fans…Again, Thank you for spending your hard earned money on an unknown. You didn't just give me a career. You gave me a dream.

Theresa Shaver

Contents

Prologue

Harry Dennison helped his wife, Anna, up into the wagon seat and handed her up the food basket when she was settled. She gave him a warm smile but he could see the quiet sorrow in her faded blue eyes. As he walked around the horses his own sorrow surfaced. He had come to terms with the deaths of his son and daughter-in-law but now that his only grandson, Quinn, was lost and possibly dead, his will to live had faded. He heaved his grief-exhausted, seventy year old body up into the trailer and patted his wife's knee before taking the reins and getting the horses moving.

It had been five days since the event that had turned all modern electronics into useless hunks of metal. The first day had been confusing but everyone had stayed calm and the town's small RCMP detachment kept everyone in order. By the end of the first day, when people started realizing that the event was much bigger than their small town, it was fear and uncertainty that kept things quiet. A late night meeting of the town's administration and police had a plan worked out. The residents had woken up the second day to find all of the businesses on Main Street locked and guarded until they could bring everyone to a town meeting. Runners on bikes and the few old vehicles that worked had been sent out to the surrounding properties and farms and everyone was urged to make their way to the community centre for a meeting.

There were many scared people yelling in the center before they finally settled down and the limited answers people had were given out. It was decided that the grocery store, two gas stations and other businesses would open at reduced hours with strict rationing policies until they could get more news from the government. They sent three of the working cars out to the north, east and south to try and find some answers. Quite a few people in town guessed correctly that there would be no help coming and they explained their thoughts to the others. There were quite a few generators that still worked and they organized water pumping stations around town and powered up the community center. People were advised to make lists of supplies on hand in their homes and anyone who would be short on food could ask for help from the town.

Once most of the townspeople had left the building, a second meeting was held with the main farm owners that had been asked to stay behind. The people in charge knew that they had to plan long term in case help wasn't coming. Harry and his neighbours were the biggest farm holders and those people were already dealing with the uncertainty of whether or not their children would be coming home from the class trip to California. Supplies and stock were listed and plans for putting in crops were discussed. Without modern farm machinery, it would be a challenge but they all had at least one piece of old machinery that was still running. If they all came together and planted each farm before moving on to the next, it could be done. They would need labour to be successful but if people wanted to eat in the future, they would have to contribute. There was plenty of animal stock and they made a schedule to rotate butchering to supply the townspeople with what they had available. It was agreed that these plans would be put on hold for three days until the scouts that were sent out came back and reported what was happening in the rest of the province. They made plans to meet again in three days for a full town meeting where everyone would be told the news and the plans to go forward.

Once the meeting broke up, the farmers gathered in the parking lot. The Andrews, the Greens, the Mathers and Susan Perry joined the Dennisons. They all had children who had gone on the class trip. With no way of knowing what was happening in the world, they were all very concerned but not yet panicked over the fate of their kids.

Mary Green put her arm around Alice Andrews and gave her a squeeze.

"Sofia got home last night. She said that Red Deer is completely at a standstill just like here. She brought a few friends from the college with her and they said that there are fires burning out of control in parts of the city. The only reason they made it out was because of that old VW Bug that Josh helped her fix up. What if this is everywhere? How are our kids going to survive in California?" she said, the last word with a sob.

Eyes filled with tears as they all contemplated the fate of their children so far away and in a place filled with millions of people all fighting for survival. It was Quinn's grandfather who broke the silence.

He cleared his throat and said in his gruff, gravelly voice, "Let's not lose sight of who we are talking about here. Our kids are strong and smart. They are resourceful and they also have help. I've known Norma Moore for decades and that woman is prepared for anything. She will have a plan and ensure those kids find refuge. Besides, Alice, have you ever known Alex to give up? She will be barking at their heels to keep them moving to safety." He made eye contact with all the other parents before proclaiming, "I will bet money that our kids are already out of the city and headed our way. That is if this event has even happened down in the south. We don't even know if the US has been affected by whatever has happened. Let's just give it a few days and wait for the scouts to come back with information before we start thinking the worst. We need to deal with the here and now. I like the idea of planning for the next couple months in case this is a long term problem. Let's get together over the next few days and compare what we have working on the farms and map out how we will do the planting. We all have horses so we should use them to travel and save the gas we have for field work or emergencies. I will hitch up my team to the old buckboard wagon and come around to collect everyone in three days for the next town meeting. We should head home now and get to work."

Josh's father nodded, "I have to pick up a friend of Josh's here in town and he's going to be staying with us until this gets sorted out. I will ride over to your place later today, Harry, and we will talk stock."

The families all went their separate ways with the hope that they would have good news when they came to town in three days. Ron Green and his wife, Mary, climbed into their daughter's restored VW bug and drove to the address that Josh had given him before he had left on his school trip. He had explained to his wife what was going on in Dara and Jake's house and what his son had asked of him. She had immediately agreed that the boy and his mother should come and stay with them.

When they got to the house they were looking for, they went up the walk and knocked on the door. There was no answer at first but Mr. Green kept knocking until the door was cracked open and he could see Jake's small face peeking through the crack.

"Jake, are you okay?" When the boy didn't answer him and just stared at him with his big grey eyes he went on. "I'm Mr. Green, Josh's dad. He asked me to come and check on you and your mom for him. Can I come in?"

The door inched open a bit further. "Is Josh with you? The TV and water doesn't work. Josh can fix it. He can fix lots of stuff!" the boy told him.

"I'm sorry, Jake, but Josh and your sister are still on their school trip so he sent me over to take care of you. Is your Mom here?"

The door opened all the way and Jake stepped back to let Josh's parents in.

"She's sleeping. She probably won't wake up until it gets dark," he told them while looking at his feet.

The Greens stepped into the house and Mrs. Green couldn't help but wrinkle her nose at the stale smell of cigarettes and wine. She took a quick glance around and bit her tongue at the dirty dishes and overflowing ashtray on the coffee table. The four empty wine bottles on the floor had her shaking her head. Next to the table was a long couch and sprawled out on it was Laura, Jake's mother, and her former friend. She looked horrible with dirty hair and pale skin. She couldn't match this person up with the friend she used to know. Laura had always had a warm inviting house and she took pride in her appearance. When she and her husband had gotten a divorce and moved into town, Mary had tried to stay in touch and help out but Laura had just seemed to drift away. Seeing her former friend in this sorry state hurt her heart. She wished now that she had tried harder to keep Laura in her life. Turning her attention to Jake, she saw him clearly for the first time. He was wearing dirty pajamas that had food stains on the front and it was obvious that he hadn't bathed in a few days. Her heart hardened at the sight of him staring longingly at the passed out figure on the couch. No matter what had happened in her life, Laura had two children who were supposed to come first.

Ron Green explained to Jake that he was going to stay with them for a while until things started working again and then sent him to get dressed and pack a bag full of clothes and a few toys he wanted to bring. When Jake had left the room, he looked at the passed out woman on the couch and then turned to his wife with a look of disgust.

"We need to try and wake her up. I'm not carrying her out of here in that state."

Mary nodded and went to the couch and tried to rouse her former friend. After shaking her and yelling at her she gave up.

"We could throw water on her but right now I'm afraid I might say some ugly things to her. How she could do this and leave her child alone to fend for himself infuriates me. From the way Jake responded, this isn't the first time she has done this. Let's just leave her to sleep it off. We will write a note and leave it on her cigarette pack. She can find her way out to our place or we can check back with her in a few days when we come back to town. I don't even know if she would realize that he is gone." She huffed out a frustrated breath and went in search of pen and paper.

Mr. Green went down the hall to help Jake pack and couldn't believe that Dara had been dealing with this. The weight on that girl's shoulders must have been huge. Now that he had seen firsthand what the situation was in this house, he was even more proud of his son for trying to take on some of that weight. He was so frustrated with the whole situation and he kept thinking that if he ever saw Jake and Dara's father again he would be hard pressed to not punch his lights out for leaving his kids to deal with this on their own.

After leaving the note where it would be impossible to miss, they took Jake out and got him into the car. They left the town without seeing another working vehicle.

The next two days were tense and stressful for all the families. They rode horses over their properties to plan with each other and make schedules for planting and butchering. They all hoped that things would clear up before they had to implement them but after the second day they all saw that it would have to happen if they wanted to feed the town and their own families. By the time Harry Dennison drove his wagon over to pick them up for the town meeting, the tension was overwhelming. Once everyone had been picked up, they rode in silence, each consumed with the thoughts of their children so far away and the fact that their farms were going to become communal property to feed the town.

Everyone was surprised to find a roadblock set up on the outskirts of town. Three men, one police officer and two men from the town were manning it with shotguns and rifles. They waved the wagon through and explained that there had been a lot of people from the highway and city walking into town and they were trying to keep a handle on who was coming in. They had sent everyone to the community center and it was starting to look like a refugee camp.

The town had changed in just the few days since the last meeting. All the dead cars had been removed from the streets and there were more people out. They were all walking towards the community center and there were more children this time. As the days had passed without official outside help, parents became more and more concerned and they kept their families close.

Harry noticed a man standing against a lamppost. He was rough-looking and stood out as he was one of the few people not walking towards the meeting. It took him a minute to place the man. The sneer on his face made it click. Hank Morris. Harry didn't know him personally but he knew the man had a reputation as a troublemaker. He had heard that Hank ran with a rough crowd and that he was a frequent visitor to the town's drunk tank. As the wagon passed him by, Hank took a last drag on his smoke and tossed it down onto the street before turning and walking in the opposite direction as everyone else. Harry shook his head and was thankful the man wouldn't be at the meeting to cause problems.

The parking lot of the center was filled with people and there were tables set up with food and water as well as a table that held huge coffee urns with electrical extension cords running back into the building. People were lined up at these tables and Harry saw that there were many that looked exhausted and filthy. Refugees from the highway or cities had walked in to the town and were just looking for a safe place with food and water. He frowned at the numbers and sighed. They would have to find a way to feed them.

There were more than a few horses already grazing in the enclosed playing field beside the center so they got theirs unhitched and led them over to the others. As the group approached the main doors, they got into line and saw that there were administrators with clipboards taking down names and addresses to form a census of who was still in the area and who would need to be fed in the coming weeks. After giving all of their names and household numbers, the entire group declined to be put on rations. They all had plenty of food on the farms and many had cellars with food that had been canned on top of the livestock.

Each of the families in the group had brought food with them to contribute to the town and they were directed to take the eggs and milk jugs to the kitchen before entering the main hall for the meeting.

There was a loud murmur coming from the crowd as they found seats and it got louder as more and more people came into the room. There was a small stage erected at the front of the hall and the Mayor, a police officer and another man that Harry recognized as Jim Johnson were standing beside it. "Big Jim" owned the only car dealership and quite a chunk of real estate in town. His normally booming voice was hushed, but by the way he punctuated his words with sharp motions of his hands, Harry knew he was unhappy.

It took another fifteen minutes before everyone was in the hall and the Mayor stood on the stage with his hands raised for attention. Once there was silence, he gave a nod at the crowd and began.

"It has been five days since the power went out. From what we have heard from others, our best guess is that an EMP or electromagnetic pulse was detonated in the atmosphere somewhere over this continent. Two of the three scouts we sent out have come back and the news they have returned with is not good. The first and most important thing they have told us is that is doesn't look like there were any bombs detonated in Alberta. Our two main cities, Edmonton and Calgary are still intact so we weren't nuked. Beyond that we don't know what is going on in the rest of the country or in the United States. They saw many fires out of control and there were quite a few crash sites where planes had gone down. Hardly anything mechanical is moving unless it is an older model or has a simple motor with no electronics in it. They report seeing a lot of ATV's and quads moving as well as some golf carts. The highways are starting to fill up with people who are fleeing the cities. Our scouts are reporting some crime but so far it seems that people are grouping up and helping each other. What they didn't see was any form of government or military presence. There were rumors on the roads that the event didn't affect anything a hundred kilometers past Edmonton so this could mean that we would see help coming from the north. That doesn't fill me with much hope as we know that there isn't a lot of population up there. The bottom line is we are on our own and we need to put into place a plan to get crops planted and the basic necessities functioning again. We have started taking a census to get a population number but as of yet, we don't have those figures yet. We know that there are a lot of people from town who commute to the city for work and many of those people have not made it back yet. We have also had many people come into town that were stuck on the highways or have walked from other areas. We will need to crunch some numbers and see how many people we can realistically feed and house with what we have and what we can grow. Once we have that number we most likely will have to turn many refugees away at the town borders."

When the Mayor paused to take a drink of water the crowd started to talk to each other and voices started to yell out questions. He held his arms up again and tried to get them to settle down. Eventually, someone blew a loud whistle and it brought silence to the room.

"Listen up, everyone! I know you have questions but we need to get through this information first and then we will try to answer questions to things we haven't covered. The first thing we need to do is get an accurate count of who is here and who isn't. If you know that some of your neighbours are missing and their homes are empty, please let the town secretaries know on your way out. We don't want abandoned homes broken into. Eventually we will have to move people into them as the community center fills up. Next we need to think about food and water. We have the supermarket locked down and it has a generator to keep the freezers going. We will ration out food from there as it is needed for as long as we can, but obviously that won't last forever. We have made a plan with all the local farms and we will let everyone know what it is at the next meeting in a week. The farm supply store had a big delivery a couple of weeks ago so all the garden seeds are in. All available green space needs to be planted. That means front yards, back yards and all public green spaces. We have to think long term, people. We may need to survive the winter on our own so the more we can grow and get canned or bottled the better. We have three water distribution sites set up around the town right now but there are things we can do to make that better. Rain can be used for cleaning and cooking so start rounding up barrels to go under downspouts. The food you have on hand should be rationed to last as long as possible. We're lucky we have the capability to grow a lot of what we need, but it won't yield for months. The next..."

The Mayor came to an abrupt halt when sounds of shouting came from outside the doors and the report of a gun going off rang out. There were a few screams from the crowd and people started to stand up. Within seconds of the gunshot, the main doors to the hall and the two sets of doors on either side were thrown open and men with shotguns, rifles and handguns rushed into the room and surrounded the people on all sides. Anyone who had been standing against the walls was shoved roughly towards the middle and many fell on the people seated in chairs. The noise in the hall was deafening with the confused and scared townspeople yelling and screaming. The wall of guns aimed at them kept anyone from trying to leave. The Mayor was yelling as loud as possible at the invaders but was silenced as a tall man climbed up onto the stage and struck him with the butt of his rifle. He turned to the crowd as a few more of his men joined him on the stage and he silenced everyone by shooting twice into the ceiling.

In the paralyzing silence that followed, he roared out, "SIT DOWN AND SHUT UP!"

Everyone dropped down into their seats or on to the floor and many parents pushed their children down onto the floor to try and shield them. The tall man on the stage gave a grim smile of satisfaction that the crowd was now under his control. He kicked the Mayor with his big boot until he rolled off the stage and then faced the crowd.

"The world is now an ugly place and my men and I have come to this town to protect it. We will be taking over the administration and security from this point on. Now, there is no such thing as a free lunch so you people will work for us to pay for that protection. This is how it will work. All the children and some of the women will be staying here in the hall for safety. They rest of you will be divided up into teams that will go out with my men and work on planting the fields and tending to the livestock around town. Anyone who decides they don't want to work or tries to run will have to deal with the consequences! If you aren't working for me then I have no reason to keep your women and children safe. Just to make this really clear, you run or fight and they DIE!" He roared the last word.

All eyes were on him as he surveyed the crowd and he had to shake his head and laugh at how easy it had been to take this town. All it had taken was one Judas to feed him the information on when they were going to have the meeting and all his new subjects were sitting ducks. The road blocks had been a joke to take over with all his men outnumbering the guards and it was smooth sailing into town. Yes, he would now be the new king to these people and life was going to get a whole lot more fun.

"So before we divide everyone up we have a few little details to sort out." He turned behind him and waved Hank Morris over to him. He held out his hand for the paper Hank was holding and took it from the smiling man before addressing the crowd again. "One of your townspeople, Hank Morris, was good enough to let us know that you needed our help and he has provided us with a list of people that will be getting a pink slip today."

He called out nine names and they included the Mayor and all of the police officers in the town as well as a few other business owners. They were all men and they were made to kneel in front of the stage.

"I am the new boss of this town and I will be in charge from this moment on. As your new boss I'm sorry to tell you men that your services are no longer needed. In other words…YOU'RE FIRED!"

Boss pulled his gun from its holster and calmly shot each of the kneeling men in the head. The crowd erupted in screams, yells and panic. The people in the first row shoved their chairs back into the people behind them and others stood and turned to run. The line of outlaws around the edge of the room all raised their guns and aimed at the panicked crowd, bringing them to a stop.

From the stage, the Boss roared out for them to return to their seats and after the execution they had just seen there was no resistance. Hank Morris was staring down at the dead men. He hated most of them and felt that he had been picked on by the police for no reason. He thought he would be happy with them dead but his plan was that he would control the town after the takeover and he was starting to see his mistake. He reached for his gun but before it could clear its holster, his arm was grabbed by one of Boss's men.

Boss looked him up and down and shook his head. "What's the matter, Hank? Did you really think you would be in charge? I run this outfit and the men all answer to me." He reached over and took the gun from Hank's holster and then turned to the crowd.

"I want all of you to know that I'm a fair man. This man betrayed you all and sold you out to me and my men. Here is a little bit of justice."

Boss didn't even look at Hank as he raised the man's gun and executed him. This time the crowd stayed silent except for some weeping and crying children.

"People of Prairie Springs, welcome to my town. Let's get to work!"

Chapter One

It had been three days since Alex and her group of friends had discovered the fate of their town. They were deep in the forest at a little used campsite and they had all sunk into depression and despair. Alex had proclaimed that they would fight to get their family and town free but none of them could agree on how to go about it. Josh wanted to go in with guns blazing; Quinn wanted to sneak people out a few at a time and Cooper was so full of guilt that he offered no suggestions at all. Dara had lost herself in misery and had hardly spoken. Alex was so frustrated that it brought her to tears and she found herself just walking away into the woods. They had all stopped talking to each other and she spent the last two days wandering the forest around their campsite wracking her brain to find a solution. Going into town head-on would just get a lot of people killed and sneaking them out wouldn't amount to anything except tipping their hand. The main advantage they had was surprise and they needed to keep it until they were ready to make their move. They needed more information. They needed to map out where everyone was in town and what farms the people were being held at. Whatever they finally did had to be planned out and implemented quickly.

She was sitting on a stump of a tree chewing on a piece of grass when she heard someone crashing through the foliage towards her. She didn't bother pulling her gun as she had been listening to Josh stomp his way through the forest for years. There was a reason she never took him hunting. Game would hear Josh coming for a mile. When he finally made it to her position he was red-faced and sweating. She just stared at him with her eyebrows raised until he got his breath back. He threw himself down on the forest floor and put his head in his hands.

"I can't do this anymore, Alex! It's been three days and all we've done is sit around and argue and mourn. Who knows what's happening to our families. We have to do something!"

Alex looked down at him and dropped the grass she had been chewing on.

"Yes. Let's go back to the others. I have some ideas."

Josh's head came up and he looked at her with hope. "Finally!"

They made their way back to the campsite where the others were all stewing in their misery.

Alex looked at them all and huffed out a breath of frustration.

"Okay, that's enough. Get over here, everyone!"

When they were all standing around the picnic table, Alex made eye contact with them all before beginning.

"Listen, I'm scared too but sitting around being depressed isn't going to help our families. I know we all feel helpless right now but I want you all to remember something. We got out of a city on fire. We found transportation home when nothing worked. We took down a group of thugs and rescued children. We made it through two countries against all odds. The reason we did all that? We didn't give up! Come on, guys! We made it home and our families need our help! I am not going to give up now, are you?"

Dara scrubbed at her head with her hands before replying.

"It's not that we are giving up, Alex. It's just...what do we do?" she asked in a defeated tone.

Alex squared her shoulders. "Well, the first thing we have to do is get out of here. Sitting here hiding isn't going to get us any closer to freeing our town. We need information. We need to map out the town and find out where everyone is. We need to scout and we need to watch the bad guys to see if we can figure out any patterns in their schedule. When do they rotate the guards? Where are they based? We can't make a plan until we have more information and we can't get that information sitting out here in the woods. So, let's start there!"

Quinn was nodding his head thoughtfully before turning and going to the camper. He came back with paper and pencils and tape. When he dropped them onto the table, he looked at the others.

"Alex is right. We need info. So let's tape this paper up into a big sheet and start drawing out the town. Tomorrow we should split up into groups and start scouting around. It will take a few days but we should have all we need to know to put a plan together. I think today we should scout out the RV resort north of town and see if we can scavenge some more supplies."

A spark was starting to spread through the group and Josh fanned it. With a trademark Josh grin, he asked,

"So, can we go all Red Dawn on their asses?"

Alex had to laugh.

"Not yet, Josh. We don't want to tip our hand, but once we know their schedule and where everyone is then yes, we will go gorilla on them!"

Josh pumped his fist in the air and whooped while doing his funky dance.

"The Maple Leaf Mafia is back in business!"

There were smiles for the first time in three days as the group gathered around the table and got to work. They all had different knowledge of the town and surrounding areas and took turns filling in the map.

They marked different approaches and places they could hide while spying on the areas they were interested in. Alex, Quinn and Josh knew all of the trails they could take in the forest close to their homes and Dara and Cooper gave details of shortcuts through town. They spent the next hour and a half working together until they had the map fleshed out to all of their satisfaction.

Alex sat back and sighed happily. It felt good to finally be doing something. She felt her belly rumble and for the first time in days felt her appetite return. She left the others at the table and went in to the camper to make some lunch. They had started making soups and stews to stretch out their supplies and she had one simmering on the stove before long. Humming to herself, she mixed a fresh batch of biscuits and popped them in to the oven. While she waited for them to bake, she did a quick inventory of their food supplies. They still had quite a bit but it wouldn't last five people more than a week and a half.

Alex liked the idea of scavenging more supplies and the RV resort was the perfect place to do it. When they had left for the school trip, there had still been some snow on the ground so most of the RVs would still be in the storage compound. There were people who winter-camped at the resort but most people started the camping season on the May long weekend. Her family owned a fifth wheel trailer and she knew that her mother left a lot of dry goods in the pantry so chances are others would as well. She even knew how to get into many of the locked campers from experience. More than once they had locked the doors in the fall and then forgotten where the keys were the following spring.

Once the soup and biscuits were ready, she carried the pot out to the table and they carefully folded the map away and had lunch. While they ate, they decided on a plan to scout out the resort. They wanted to bring back as much as possible but they also wanted to be quiet. Their best defence was being able to hear a vehicle coming in time to hide. They decided to put their bikes in the back of the truck and take it as close to the resort as they could before biking in the rest of the way. They could make trips back to the truck with the supplies they found. After seeing what was going on in the town, they were very cautious and each of the teens carried a handgun and an assault rifle with extra ammunition. A backpack with a small amount of food, water bottles and a first aid kit was also packed. They piled into the truck with Quinn driving and Alex in the passenger seat. The others climbed into the bed with the bikes and they drove slowly back towards the road leading into their secluded campsite.

The resort was huge, with over four hundred camping sites, a small store and pool. The storage compound had at least three hundred campers of all different makes and models and it would be a great source of supplies if it hadn't already been looted. There was a paved road running between the area where the kids were camped and the resort and as they came up to it, Quinn came to a stop and shut the engine off. Josh hopped over the side of the truck and made his way up to the pavement. After listening for sounds and hearing nothing, he moved out onto it and scanned both ways before waving Quinn through.

Quinn drove over the pavement and on to the gravel access road that led deeper into the forest and the resort. Josh hopped back in and they followed the road slowly. Alex leaned forward and watched for the turn they wanted. She knew there was a service road that skirted the resort and that's where they were going to hide the truck. The main highway that ran through town wasn't very far away to the south but with the trees between them they would be out of sight.

Quinn pulled over off the road and shut the engine off. They all piled out and Josh started to hand down the bikes. Alex scanned the area around them and was going over the resort's layout in her head when a sound caught her attention. Her head came up and she looked to the west and held up her hand. Everyone froze and strained to hear what she had.

Josh was still standing in the bed of the truck and he turned towards the trees separating them from the highway.

"Two engines maybe, but not cars or trucks, something smaller. They're coming from the west, I think," he reported in a low voice. "It could be our bad guys scouting or it could be people heading to town who don't know what's waiting for them." He turned and looked down at the others. "Should we check it out? We can cut straight through here and stay under cover but still be able to see the highway."

Quinn looked at Alex and the others and everyone nodded. They needed information and now was as good a time as any to start getting it. Dara leaned her bike against the truck and Josh jumped down. All together they entered the trees and moved south towards the road. They were only ten feet from the edge of the trees and they could see glimpses of the pavement when the sound of multiple engines drowned out the first ones they had heard. Alex moved a few more feet forward and dropped down into a crouch before moving right to the edge of the trees. All that separated her from the road was a grass-filled ditch. Scanning right and left she saw two ATVs slow down to a stop while two old trucks and four motorcycles blocked the road ahead of them. The teens were behind the trucks by about fifteen feet and it was clear to Alex that they were part of the outlaws holding her town. She scooted back into the woods and paralleled the road to get a better look at who was on the ATVs. When she got a good look at the girl with long blond hair climbing off of the lead four-wheeler, she almost gave them away. Alex rocked to her feet and opened her mouth to shout. Before any sound came out, Quinn had her by the arm and was covering her mouth. She turned horror-filled eyes towards him and he gave a grim nod.

The hand he had covering her mouth pulled away and he gently stroked her face before turning to the others.

"It's Emily and the other group. We are not letting those bastards take them into town! Josh, Cooper, go back down the road and cut across to the other side. They're all looking ahead so they shouldn't see you. As soon as you get across, book it back this way and get ahead of them but stay under cover. Alex, Dara and I will move up on this side. Be ready. We're going to have to take these guys out. We can't let them get back to town or they will all be hunting for us. Watch where you're shooting, we don't want to get caught in the crossfire and shoot each other. Go!"

Josh and Cooper took off without a word and Quinn pulled Alex down into a crouch. Dara joined them and they moved quickly back into the woods and then forwards until they were opposite Emily and the others on the road. Quinn patted Dara on the shoulder and pointed where he wanted her. She gave a brief nod and squeezed Alex's hand before belly-crawling into position. Quinn pointed out where he wanted Alex and then pointed to himself and showed her where he would be. She nodded with grim determination and crawled away.

When she got to the edge of the trees, she glanced over to the road before she was going to crawl into the tall grass of the ditch. What she saw froze her. A man with long dirty hair was standing in front of Emily and pointing a gun at her.

"Get into the truck!" he roared at Emily.

Alex could only hope that everyone was in position and ready because she wasn't going to wait a second longer.

"I'm pretty sure she doesn't want to go anywhere with someone as ugly as you!" she taunted as she stood up and swung her rifle towards him.

All heads turned and stared at her. She stood tall and glared fiercely at him. His gun swung towards her and he gave her a creepy smile before calling out to his men.

"Well, what do you know? Look, guys, we got another pretty little girl to join the party!" he gave a nasty laugh as he scanned Alex's body up and down.

His smile turned grim when a voice called out from the other side of the road.

"Hey! It's really stupid to tease a redhead with a big gun, mister. If I was you, I'd duck and cover 'cause she looks pissed!"

Alex could see the calculation in the long haired man's eyes. She took a quick glimpse behind him and saw the other men were spreading out. Looking back at the long haired man, she saw his confidence bloom and he called out,

"Don't worry, buddy. She'll be playing with my big gun soon enough!"

Alex's body tensed and she tightened her finger on the trigger. They were out of time. She hoped everyone was ready. She opened her mouth to yell but before she had time, she caught movement from the corner of her eye. Her mouth dropped open in shock as she watched her sweet natured best friend raise her arm and shoot the man threatening them.

Everything seemed to slow down in that moment. She saw Emily drop the gun on the ground before being tackled by David. Alex heard the sound of Emily's head hitting the pavement in the split second before the explosive sound of multiple guns started firing. She turned her head and saw the long haired man frozen with a look of disbelief on his face before crumpling to the road. With him down, she had a clear view of what was happening with the others. The bad guys were firing at both sides of the road into the forest and she saw them fall one by one until there was only one man left hiding between the trucks. She had a straight shot at him so she lined up the rifle and took him out.

A screech of pain had her whipping her head to the side. Mason was on the ground holding his face. Blood was gushing in between his fingers to drip onto the road. Lisa was the one screeching. She was clawing at a man who was pulling her towards the ditch by her long chestnut brown hair. She was being dragged on her bottom across the road and couldn't get a purchase with her feet. The man's face was filled with desperation and he was frantic to make it to the ditch with his prize to use as a shield.

Alex turned the rest of her body to face them and brought her rifle to bear. She screamed at Lisa.

"DROP FLAT!!!"

Lisa went limp and the man was left exposed with nothing but her long hair in his hand. Alex didn't even have time for a shot before three bullets from three different guns struck him in the chest. His hand spasmed open and her head dropped to the pavement with a thunk before he toppled backwards.

There was dead silence for a few seconds. Even nature had held her breath while the birds and insects had disappeared. Quinn suddenly called out,

"How many down?"

Alex had the best view of the carnage they had created and she started to shake as she counted the fallen men. Her voice was shaky as she called out,

"Seven."

Quinn launched himself from the tall grass and started to scan his friends frantically.

"Was anyone hit?!"

Everyone called out as they moved on to the road. Josh was bleeding from his arm but it was a shallow graze and he waved it off with a grimace. Dara had two nicks on her face from tree bark fragments that had ricocheted. Mason seemed to be the most damaged. He had taken a hard punch to the face from the man who had grabbed Lisa and it looked like his nose was broken. Lisa was laying on the road in a ball, sobbing, and Emily was also down. It looked like she was unconscious. David had rolled off of her and was scanning around for any other danger. When he saw that they were safe, he turned back to Emily and started to feel the back of her head. His face was filled with relief, when all he found was a goose egg from her fall.

Alex was about to rush to her when Quinn grabbed her arm.

"David, is she okay?"

"Yeah, but she's going to have a huge headache when she wakes up."

Quinn nodded. "Okay, we need to get this cleaned up and get out of here! Anyone could have heard those shots. If we want to stay hidden from town, then we need to move fast!" He turned to Josh, Dara and Cooper, "We need to pull the bodies into the woods and dump the motorcycles in there too. We can drive the trucks and ditch them somewhere else. If we can clean this up like it never happened then maybe the gang in town will just think these guys took off or something and it's seven less bad guys we have to worry about later. Let's get to work. I don't want to be standing out here if anyone else shows up!"

Josh and Cooper went straight to the first body and grabbed it by the arms and feet before staggering down into the ditch and into the trees. Dara went to the motorcycles and started pushing one into the woods as well.

David was looking at them in confusion and the other three were still out of it.

"What's going on, Quinn?"

Alex and Quinn had just picked up a body and he grunted out, "No time right now, David. Just get the others into one of the trucks and then help us!"

They staggered down into the ditch and moved into the trees.

David didn't know what was happening but he had just witnessed his lifelong friends kill seven men. He got Emily up over his shoulder and carried her to the first truck he came to. Once he had her inside and buckled up he went back for Lisa and Mason.

Mason was still on his knees clutching his face so David stripped off his shirt and balled it up.

"Mason, Mason look at me!"

When Mason lifted his head David saw the tears streaming down the boy's face. He offered his balled up shirt to him to press against his nose but Mason just shook his head.

"I dink my ose is oken."

He grabbed his nose and gave it a yank. The sound it made straightening out made David want to gag. Mason took David's proffered shirt and held it against his nose while looking around at the bodies on the road.

"What just appened?" he asked.

David shook his head and headed over to get Lisa up and moving. She was still rolled up in a ball, crying on the pavement.

"I have no idea except they seem to think that more bad guys might be coming, so let's help them clear the road."

Lisa staggered against him as he led her over to the truck and helped her slide in next to Emily. After everything that had happened on the way home, it seemed she had finally broken down. He shut the door and joined Mason at the closest body. They heaved him up and carried him into the trees and dumped him. David knew he should be appalled by this but his emotions seemed to be flat at the moment. Twenty minutes ago he was so excited and hopeful that they had almost made it home and now he wasn't sure if there was a home to go to.

When they return to the road, he saw Quinn and Cooper carrying the second last body into the trees, and Dara and Josh are each pushing a motorcycle down into the ditch. He looked over toward the last body and saw it was the man that Emily shot lying facedown on the road. Rage filled him. This disgusting man ruined the happy homecoming that he thought they would have so he used his boot to roughly flip him over. The burning, hateful eyes were all the warning David needed to dive to one side as the long haired man pulled the trigger of the gun he had been holding under his body. The minute he landed on the gravel on the side of the road, his hands started patting the ground looking for something to defend himself with. He came up with a fist-sized rock, and with all his adrenaline-fueled rage, brought it down on the weakened man's head. David was mindless with fury and kept hitting the man until strong hands pulled him off.

"David, David! Stop, STOP!!!" Josh was shaking him and when he saw David's eyes focus, he let go and stepped back. "He's dead, David."

David's chest heaved as he tried to calm down. He looked down at the mangled mess of the long haired man's face and staggered away to vomit into the ditch. He just killed a man with his bare hands. He held his hands in front of his face and saw they were covered in blood. He wasn't sure they would ever be clean again.

Alex's voice had him turning around.

"Oh my God! Oh no, NO!"

David looked at her crumpled face and followed her line of sight. Lying on the road with his arms thrown wide was Mason. If the small blot of blood directly over his heart wasn't enough evidence then his wide open, empty eyes were. Mason was dead.

Chapter Two

David's face drained of colour and he looked away. They had come so far, they were steps from home and their families and Mason was dead. He shot a glance over at the truck and saw that Lisa and Emily were still oblivious to what was happening. His mind couldn't process how this had happened. He looked to his friends for help but they all stood staring down at Mason. Quinn finally shook his head.

"We have to go. We can't stay here. Josh, will you help me get Mason into the back of one of the trucks? We can give him a proper burial somewhere else."

The two boys picked Mason up and when David made to follow them, Alex grabbed his arm.

"I'm so sorry, David."

He looked at her blankly.

"I don't understand this. What's going on? Why are you guys out here with those guns? Where are all the adults?"

She rubbed his arm while guiding him to an empty truck.

"I know you're confused right now, but something has happened in town, and it's not safe for us to go there. We'll explain everything when we get back to our campsite. We need to get this road cleaned up and get out of here before more bad guys show up. Just get in. Dara will drive this truck and I'll drive the other one back. Quinn and Cooper will bring the ATV's you guys were riding on and Josh is going to go get our truck that we left on the other side of those trees. I promise we will explain everything when we get to safety."

David let himself be led as he climbed into the truck and stared out at the empty road. All he knew was that he wanted to go home.

Alex ran over to the last body and helped Quinn drag it into the trees. When they came out, Cooper was dumping a huge jug of water over the bloodstains on the road. She looked at Quinn with a question.

"There were two water jugs in the back of the truck so we're trying to wash some of the blood off of the road. It won't clean it all but it might dilute it enough that once it dries, no one will notice it right away. Anything we can do to keep the bad guys from knowing we took out their men will help keep us hidden." He scanned the road and nodded, "Okay, I think that's about all we can do so let's head back to the campsite. We need to regroup and make a new plan."

He pulled her close for a brief hug and then walked over to the ATV that David had been driving when they had run into trouble.

Alex jumped into the truck with the girls and was relieved to see the peaceful face of her best friend. The longer Emily was out, the longer it was until she had to tell her that her boyfriend was dead. Alex knew it was an awful thing to think, but she was a little bit surprised that Lisa and Mason had made it home at all. That thought made her realize that Mark was missing. She wondered what had happened to him and glanced over at Lisa. The girl had her eyes closed and she was leaning against Emily. Alex wondered what their journey home had been like and if they had faced as many hardships as her group had. Movement caught her eye and she saw Josh run down the ditch and disappear into the trees towards the service road they had parked on. Dara moved ahead in the other truck and flipped a U-turn so Alex followed and they quickly headed back to the campsite.

The drive back was uneventful and Alex kept stealing glances at her best friend. She was so happy to see Emily and David but was filled with dread at having to tell them what was going on in their town. That news on top of Mason's death was going to destroy her friend. She sneaked another peek and was surprised to see Lisa staring back. The girl was as beautiful as ever, but there seemed to be something different about her. The superior air and disdain that usually filled her eyes was gone. In its place was a deep sadness.

"Are you okay?"

Lisa slowly nodded her head before asking, "Are things just as bad here?"

Alex tried to find the right words but came up blank so she just nodded. Lisa sighed and turned her head to look out at the trees passing by. As they came to the clearing where they had setup camp, Emily let out a groan and brought her hand up to her head. Alex brought the truck to a stop behind Dara and quickly turned to Emily.

"It's okay, you're safe."

"What happened? My head is killing me!" Emily's hazy eyes focused on Alex and grew wide, "Alex! Oh my God, Alex, I didn't think I would ever see you again!" Tears started to flow down her face as the two girls embraced.

Emily sobbed into Alex's shoulder and Alex just held her tight. She saw Lisa sitting quietly, watching them, and the girl's eyes were also filled with tears so Alex reached over and pulled Lisa into the hug as well. No matter what had happened before the pulse, they were all survivors and she deserved a hug too.

The door behind Lisa was suddenly pulled open and David stood there frantically looking Emily over. When he saw that she was fine, he stepped back and took a deep breath. The girls separated and wiped tears from their faces before getting out of the truck. Alex guided them over to the picnic table as Quinn, Cooper and Josh pulled up behind the two stolen trucks.

Josh swaggered over with a grin and slapped David into a one-armed hug. He looked around at the group and laughed.

"Look at this! We made it! The world stopped and we made it across two countries and have a parking lot full of vehicles that work. Hot damn, we're good!"

Alex had to smile at his antics. He was right, they were so lucky to have made it this far and have some resources. Her smile widened at having her whole group of friends back together. She squeezed Emily's hand and turned to David. The look on his face was enough to wipe the smile off of her face. He stared back at them with incredulous anger before he launched into a rant.

"We didn't all make it!" he spat at Josh. "What the hell were you guys doing? The way you came out of the trees with your big guns blazing was insane! You killed all those people like it was nothing. You didn't even try to talk to them! What happened to you guys? Is this who you are now, pretend-soldiers who go around and gun people down?" His face was flushed red and filled with contempt.

Quinn stepped forward and held up his hand. "Easy, David, you don't know what's happening here. I'm sorry about Mason but those men we killed would have really messed you guys up if we hadn't stopped them!"

"Mason? What happened to Mason? Where's Mason?" Emily suddenly stood up and started to look around in confusion.

David rushed to her and took her hands. "I'm so sorry, Emily. One of the men shot him. He didn't make it."

Emily stared into David's eyes and when she saw the compassion there, she made a small "oh" sound and crumpled back onto the bench. She pulled away from David and turned to pull Lisa into her arms.

"So close, we were so close!" she cried.

Lisa held on to Emily but her eyes were clear of tears. There was only so much a person could take before they hardened and their emotions became blunted. Part of her was sad that Mason had died, but mostly she felt a cold ball of anger in her core.

David spun back to the group. "This is your fault! We could have talked to them or you could have held your guns on them while we escaped! If you hadn't just opened fire, Mason wouldn't have been shot!"

Emily pulled back from Lisa and stood up, placing her hand on David's arm.

"David, it's my fault, not theirs. I fired the first shot when that man threatened Alex. This is all my fault," she said sadly, looking at the ground.

Before he could respond, Quinn stepped in again.

"Listen, those men have taken over our town. They have our families as hostages and they are using them as slave labour. We will have to fight them anyway. This was just the first battle we'll have to fight."

David pulled away from Emily and paced away. His face was anguished and he was pulling on his hair.

"This is insane! This can't be happening!" he muttered before swinging back to the group and zeroing in on Quinn and yelling, "What is wrong with you? This isn't your job! Have you forgotten that we are just teenagers? We can't just go wage war. We aren't soldiers!" He paused and looked frantically at everyone's faces. "I killed him! I KILLED THAT MAN!"

There was dead silence in the clearing as everyone watched the horror and pain on David's face. Everyone knew exactly what he was feeling. They had all taken a life to get this far and they knew that they would carry that burden for the rest of their lives.

David was hunched over with his arms wrapped around his mid-section. Everyone could see the painful struggle he was going through but no one made a move to go to him. They knew it was something he needed to come to terms with on his own. Each and every one of them had taken a life and the consequences had come after the fact with nightmares and depression. It was finally Lisa who stood up and broke the silence.

"Quinn, is there any help at all? Any police, military…adults that can help us?"

When he shook his head, her face hardened and she turned to face David.

"This is it. We are it. If we want to go home, we have to fight! David, you saw what things are like out there. I mean, we walked through it! Taking a life is a horrible thing. I almost ended mine after Mark, but Emily made me see that I did what I had to do to survive. We can fold up and collapse, or we can be soldiers and fight for our lives and our families lives! I know this is hard but I am going to fight and I hope you will help us."

She turned back to Quinn and ignored the surprised look on his face. She knew what Alex and her friends thought of her, but she wasn't that shallow cheerleader anymore and they would have to figure that out for themselves.

"Do you have a shovel? I would like to bury Mason," she asked him.

Quinn was shocked at the difference in Lisa and had to wonder what she had meant about "after Mark". He noticed Mark hadn't come home with them, but he didn't know what had happened to him. Before he could answer her, Cooper stepped up and offered to help. She nodded and walked away from the group. Dara jumped up and went to the camper to get a sheet to wrap the body in.

Emily went to David and wrapped him in her arms, trying to comfort him as best as she could. Alex watched them for a moment before meeting Quinn's eyes.

She huffed out a breath. "We have a lot to talk about but I think we should take care of Mason and then put a meal together. We can share our stories after that and then make some plans."

Quinn nodded his agreement and they left to help the others with Mason's body. Josh was the only one left at the table and he watched David and Emily. He was a little surprised that Emily wasn't more broken up about Mason's death. The last time he had seen them at Disneyland she was the guy's girlfriend, but the way she was holding on to David and kissing his face showed him that things had changed.

Josh gave a small sad smile. Whatever they had faced on the way home had changed them and although he was happy his friend had gotten the girl he was in love with, he knew that it would always be tainted with sadness from the event that had changed all their lives.

He walked over and patted David's back. "Man, I'm really sorry about the crappy homecoming but it's so good to have you guys here."

When David just nodded, Josh turned and went to help the others.

Quinn, Josh and Cooper took turns digging the grave until they felt it was deep enough. Dara and Lisa wrapped Mason's body in a bedsheet and Alex walked around the clearing they had chosen and picked early spring flowers. She kept stealing glances at Lisa. The girl moved mechanically and had not shed any tears for the boy she had been friends with. Alex didn't know what they had gone through but it was clear that Lisa was not the same person that Alex had known before.

Once they were ready, Josh led Emily and David to the clearing and they lowered Mason down into the grave. Alex passed the flowers to Emily and Lisa and stood back waiting. David had gotten his emotions under control and he finally stepped forward.

"Mason Johnson was..." David began but ended just as quickly. He looked around at the group, at a loss for words. The silence began to drag until Lisa started to speak.

"Mason Johnson was a jerk! He was shallow and egotistical and selfish...but he was changing! He was learning what is important in life and he was trying to be a better person. I'm so very sad that he didn't get the chance to become the person that he wanted to be." She looked at the others and sighed.

"Goodbye, Mason." Dropping the flowers down into the grave, she then turned and walked away.

Emily nodded slowly and then threw the flowers she was holding down to join Lisa's.

"Goodbye, Mason. I'm sorry you didn't make it and thank you for trying to be a better person."

David tossed his flowers. "We weren't friends but we could have been. I'm sorry."

When he didn't say anything else, the rest of the group added their flowers and Quinn started to refill the grave. David and Emily were numb from the day's events and they stood quietly watching until the grave was filled in. Then they walked back to the campsite with the others.

David and Emily sat holding hands at the picnic table as Quinn and Alex filled them in on what they knew was happening in their town. Lisa stood rigid as she took in their words. They explained their plans to scout the town and farms and they showed them the map that they wanted to fill in with locations and guards. As they talked, Dara and Josh got food from the camper and started to make a meal. By the time they had finished eating, Alex had told them the story of their journey overland and David and Emily had filled them in on their own story. When they had gotten to the part about Mark, Lisa had to get up and leave the table. She didn't want to hear about Mark and what he had done to her or how she had killed him.

Lisa was struggling with inner turmoil. So many things had changed in the last month and she didn't know who she was anymore. The cheerleader was dead, but the girl she had tried to be on the way home didn't fit this new reality either. After walking round the campsite a few times she asked Alex if she could use the camper to clean up.

As she looked around at the interior of the camper and all the supplies it was filled with, she couldn't help but think how much easier the trip in from the coast would have been with a setup like this. She pushed the thought away. They had made it so that was all that mattered. Then she remembered that they hadn't all made it.

She entered the tiny bathroom and caught sight of herself in the mirror. The girl looking back at her was a stranger. The long glossy hair she was used to was tangled and matted and the cat green eyes that used to spark and flash were dull and filled with sadness. She felt so lost and wished she could cry, but there was a great emptiness inside of her. Who was she now? She had thought that she would learn to contribute and be a good person, but now there was a war and she would have to fight. Shaking her head at her image she wondered if she could do it. Killing Mark had been a desperate move to save herself and the others. Could she fight knowing that she would have to kill on a premeditated basis?

The girl in the mirror could barely hold her head up. She reached up and rubbed the aching place on her scalp. The man on the road had pulled her by the hair like it was a leash and he had torn out a handful by the roots. As she looked into the mirror, a ball of heat filled the emptiness inside of her. She had been used and assaulted and she had made a vow to never let it happen again. Until she was safe, and they had gotten their town and homes back, she would do whatever it took to stay alive and free, and she knew just where to start.

Lisa whirled away from the mirror and left the bathroom. She searched the drawers in the kitchen until she found what she was looking for and carried them back into the bathroom. She met her steely-eyed stare in the mirror and nodded at herself in determination before grabbing a hank of hair and brutally slicing through it with the scissors she had found. If she was going to be a different person she would start with how she looked. No one would be able to use her hair against her again. She hacked away as best as she could with the dull blades and never noticed the tears that were finally flowing down her face. Shocked words brought her back to herself and she stopped in mid-cut. Turning her head slowly, she saw Dara standing there staring at her with an open mouth.

"Whoa, whoa, what are you doing?!" she gasped.

When Lisa just stared at her blankly, Dara scanned the hair covered floor around her and then looked back up at her. Understanding and compassion flowed into her eyes.

"Let me help you," she said quietly.

Lisa handed the scissors to Dara and let herself be led over to the table where Dara gently pushed her down on to the bench seat. Dara grabbed a towel and draped it around Lisa's shoulders before asking, "How much?"

Lisa swallowed and whispered, "All of it."

Dara stared at her intently before nodding and moved behind her where she started to snip away at the ragged mess. She didn't speak at first and the only sound in the camper was the sound of the blades snipping. As Lisa gradually relaxed, Dara finally started to speak.

"I understand why you want this. I dyed my hair black and put in blue streaks because I couldn't stand to look at myself in the mirror. I didn't recognize the person I was anymore. When my dad left, my mother started to drink. She would get wasted and stay that way for days. My whole life changed. I had to take care of my brother and clean up my mom and the girl I used to be just disappeared. I didn't know who I was anymore so I changed my hair and made it harsh because I felt like it was the only thing I could control and it expressed how angry I was. It also helped to isolate me from others because I didn't want anyone to know what was going on with me. All anyone saw was a Goth chick and they left me alone. I know it's not quite the same as what you are going through, but I do understand."

Dara moved around in front of Lisa and after a few more snips stood back and sighed. The sound brought Lisa's head up and Dara smiled when their eyes met.

"I know you are feeling lost right now, but you are here with us and you are a survivor. You're part of our family now and we *will* get our homes back." She

~ 24 ~

paused and shook her head and then laughed. "But I have to tell you that I hate you on principle." When Lisa's eyes widened in dismay, Dara laughed again. "Here you are dirty and with all your hair chopped off and you *still* look like a supermodel!" A slow smile spread across Lisa's face and she reached out and took Dara's hand and gave it a squeeze.

"Thank you. Thank you for understanding." She rubbed her hands over her shorn head and laughed. "I feel lighter and kind of naked!"

Dara laughed, "You really do look great. Your eyes and cheekbones are killer with that cut. If you want to know the truth…you look like you could kick some serious butt!"

Lisa beamed at Dara, "That's what I want! I don't want to be a victim anymore. I want to help fight for our town and families."

Dara nodded in understanding. "Well, if a haircut was all it would take to win them back, yours would do it. Come on, let's get this cleaned up. If you want we can gather all your hair up and burn it as a symbolic gesture to becoming a new you. Then I could put warpaint on your face and send you off to destroy the bad guys!" she joked.

Lisa had to laugh at the image but she turned serious before getting up. "I'm sorry, Dara. I'm sorry I treated you so badly back in school. I was a real bitch to a lot of people. I'm not that person anymore so thank you for being nice to me."

Dara reached down and pulled Lisa to her feet. "None of us are the people we were in high school, Lisa. In a lot of ways we are better people because of all of this. Come on, let's go shock everyone and teach you how to use a gun!"

Lisa shivered at that but then squared her shoulders. She was ready to fight.

~ 25 ~

Shock was exactly what they got when they left the camper. There were double takes and mouths dropped in awe. Lisa couldn't help but blush as all eyes stared at her and she kept reaching up to touch the downy soft hair that was left. She made her way over to the picnic table where the homemade map was spread out. She lowered her head over it and studied it to avoid the attention. Emily came over and touched her hand. When Lisa looked up her friend was smiling.

"I love it. You look amazing and fierce."

Lisa smiled back but was jolted by a wolf whistle. Josh stood on the other side of the table with his goofy grin.

"Wow, Lisa, I'm not ashamed to tell you that you scared me a little bit before all this happened, but now you terrify me! I can see you with two pistols strapped to your thighs and red, red lipstick. Kicking ass and taking names. Damn girl, you look hard core dangerous!"

She was laughing and shaking her head at his over the top compliment. "I just want to help fight and being dragged around by my hair is not very helpful," she explained.

Josh was nodding emphatically. "Just nail them with that disdainful look you have patented, and they will run away whimpering!"

Lisa blushed again and turned back to the map.

"Can I help with this? There are a lot of walkways that run between and behind these houses that we might be able to use." She ran her finger over the map through the areas she was referring to.

Quinn had stepped up to the table and was nodding his head.

"Anything you can fill in is helpful; the more detailed the better. Who knows when we might need a quick getaway? From what Cooper found out, we don't think these guys are local so this is our home turf and that will give us a small advantage." He looked around at the others and then up at the dimming sky. "I think we should stay put for today and lay out what we want to do tomorrow. We still need to search for supplies at the campground and we are going to need more shelter for all of us. I think we should find somewhere in that storage compound to hide at least one of those trucks and it would be nice if we can bring back another small camper so we all have a decent place to sleep. We will also need more food." Quinn paused for a moment in thought before continuing.

"We all agreed that rushing into town was a bad idea and we planned on scouting out where everyone is and trying to get a rough estimate of how many men are holding the town. We need information and I think the longer we take to find these things out, the harder it will be on all of us so…I think we need to split up. We should split into teams of two and take different areas of the town and farms where people are being held. Another team should hit the resort and get as many supplies as they can. What do you guys think?"

Everyone was standing around the table at that point and there were serious nods all around. Cooper looked at the map before offering his opinion.

"I agree. If what Buddy said was true, then almost everyone in town will be at the community center so we should be able to sneak around without too much trouble. It would be great if we could find out where these guys are staying. I think that I should go into town with Dara. We both know our way around and we know how to get out on the pathways if we need too." He looked to Dara who was nodding. They had both spent many years walking the town as they didn't have parents who were interested in driving them around. They would make the best team to scout it out.

Alex looked at Quinn and frowned. "Quinn, I think you are going to have to do the resort. Your leg is much better but it's not up to running and crouching. You should take Lisa and get the supplies. Hopefully you guys won't have any trouble but the resort looked pretty deserted. You should be okay in there with just the two of you.

"Josh, David, Emily and I will scout the farms. I think David and I should be a team and Josh and Emily should pair up."

David frowned and started to shake his head as he put his arm around Emily. Before he could protest, Alex explained.

"David, Josh and I have more experience with the assault rifles and we've been in a few shootouts now. I know you guys had just as hard of a time getting back here but this morning was the first time you have had to deal with these types of people and I can't stand the thought of losing you guys. Both you and Emily can handle a rifle but if something goes wrong it would be better if there was a gun with more stopping power with you. I also think that Josh and I have a better handle on what needs to be done if we do get caught," she said the last softly.

David looked at her in disbelief. "So what, you guys are hard core killers now? Give me a break!"

Alex felt her cheeks grow hot at his words. She loved David like a brother, but he had no idea what he was talking about. After hearing about their journey home, she knew he hadn't had to handle very much violence. Emily and Lisa had. She stared him down until he had to look away.

"David, I know what happened this morning was hard on you and I'm sorry we are now in a world that is filled with violence. None of us are 'hard core killers'; we are survivors. Here is the reality that you need to face. Those men holding our family are using them as slaves and probably doing evil things to them. I know those types of men because I have already killed many of them. They are not going to sit down and have a chat with us and then let us go. We will have to fight them and likely kill some or all of them to free our families. If you can't handle that then you need to stay here and let us get the job done."

David's face was pale at her words and Emily turned and cupped her hand alongside of his face. When his eyes met hers, they were filled with sorrow.

"Listen to me, David. I have killed three men in the last month and every one of them wanted to hurt me. A piece of my soul will always carry a scar from it but I can live with that. We didn't do anything wrong and we are good people. These men aren't. They prey on the weak and innocent and they need to be stopped. There's no one coming to help us, so it's up to us to do it. If I have to, I will kill every single one of them to free and protect my family and friends. Alex is right. You don't have to go with us but you also need to remember that your mother and sister are in that town and if you get caught by those men because you couldn't bring yourself to kill them, then they will have one less person fighting to free them."

David leaned in and kissed Emily on the forehead before turning to his friends.

"My father was a soldier. He told me once that he joined the military because he wanted to do the right thing and help others. What he saw and what he did…it broke him. He couldn't handle what came after. The memories never left him and they destroyed him. I, I don't want that to happen to me or to any of us. I don't want us to be broken."

No one in the group could reply to that. They already felt the effects of their actions and knew it would only get worse as they fought and killed to free the town. The silence was heavy until Josh lifted his head and spoke.

"I'll take that chance." Everyone looked at him. "I will take that chance to make sure my mother and my sister are not broken. If they are safe then whatever happens to me will be worth it."

Alex started to nod and she looked at David.

"It's worth it."

Emily squeezed David's hand.

"It's worth it."

One by one they all voiced their commitment to doing whatever it took to free their loved ones. David looked at all his childhood friends and the two new ones who had joined them. He thought about his dad and wondered if he had thought it had been worth it. Then he thought about his mom and his little sister, Emma. He pictured them scared and cowering in a corner while they were being threatened by the men who were controlling the town. He felt his heart harden and he realized he *would* do anything to protect them. He looked around and met the eyes of everyone in his group. He nodded his head.

"It's worth it."

Chapter Three

Alex looked around the forest and closed her eyes and breathed deeply. The spring smell of new growth was sweet and she had never felt so close to her home. She had spent so many years playing in this area that she felt like she knew every tree and bush. She opened her eyes and shot a grin of delight at her best friend. Emily smiled back knowing exactly what Alex was feeling. They had spent so much time running through this area as kids and later as teens. It would be easy to forget what was happening in the fields ahead. They had left the bikes further back as the trail thinned out and walked the rest of the way. David was supposed to scout out the area with Alex but the two girls had decided to go together. They had always been a team and after such a long time apart, they couldn't bear to be separated again.

The trail widened ahead and they both slowed and crouched down. The clearing ahead was very well known to the two girls. After carefully checking to make sure it was empty, they scanned upwards into the trees. On the other side of the clearing, they could make out the faint outline of a homemade ladder nailed into one of the biggest trees. The watched for a few minutes and listened for any sound coming from above. When they detected nothing out of place, they moved forward and climbed the ladder up into their tree house. As soon as they entered it, they knew someone had been there. In one corner there was a tarp and it was covering something that didn't belong in the tree house. Alex held up a hand to Emily and motioned with her hand that she was going back out the door to circle around the balcony. Emily nodded and went to one of the two windows as lookout and held her rifle ready. Alex slipped back out the door and made her way around the house peering over the half railing they had completed last summer.

The tree house had gone through many transformations as they had grown up. It had started with a sloppy lean to against the trunk to gradually raising higher and higher with their ages and capabilities. The latest version was started the summer they were fourteen and involved many ladders and much hauling of wood planks. They had used a pulley system to get the boards up into the thick branches and had built the floor out into a twelve foot platform before building the walls up and around the branches. Last summer they had added a narrow balcony all the way around the house and erected the half railing for safety. Alex and her friends had worked hard to create the tree house and she remembered how proud they had been when they invited their families out into the woods to see the completed project. She felt a pang of longing when she remembered her and Josh's dad climbing all over it as he inspected every board to make sure it was secure, while Quinn's grandfather had stood on the forest floor nodding his head in approval. The few tweaks his father had suggested had made the roof waterproof and they had a mini celebration picnic.

Alex completed the inspection around the balcony and didn't find anything else out of place so she entered the house and the girls moved over to the tarp to see what was under it. Pulling the tarp aside, they saw two plastic bins and two garbage bags that had been tied off. Opening the two bins they were confused to find all of their camping gear. Alex recognized items that belonged to Quinn and Josh as well as gear that she used. The garbage bags also held their sleeping bags and two tents. Emily leaned back and frowned thoughtfully.

"It had to be one of our fathers that put this stuff here but why? They knew we wouldn't be using it so why bring it out here?"

Alex stared at the bins for a moment before reaching in and pulling gear out. When she got half of it emptied, she found food and water. Nodding her head she looked at Emily with a frown.

"It's a fallback point. They cached this stuff in case they had to leave the houses. They used our stuff because they didn't know if we would be back and they were using their gear at home. I just can't believe that none of our families got away!"

They quickly repacked the bins and covered them back up with the tarp. They had all they needed back at their campsite and they wanted to leave the supplies here in case someone from their families managed to get away and needed it. Alex contemplated leaving a note in the bin but decided it would be too much of a risk if someone else found it.

"Let's have something to eat before we go any further. We could be stuck in place for a while depending on what we find."

Emily nodded and pulled out a couple of granola bars and some beef jerky before settling on one of the camp chairs that she took down from the wall. Alex studied her friend while they ate. It was so good to have Emily back but she could tell that her friend was different. She was more quiet and watchful and there was a ghost of sadness that came and went from her eyes. The biggest change though was Emily and David being together.

"Soooooo...David?" Alex asked in a teasing tone.

Emily's cheeks turned pink and a soft smile came across her face.

"I was so blind, Alex. David was such a rock for me through the journey home. I don't know why I didn't see him like that before. I was just so caught up in Mason that it didn't even come to mind. It took so many horrible things happening for me to finally see what was right in front of me all along."

"Well, I'm happy you finally realized he is the one for you! I'm so happy you're here, Em," Alex said.

Emily nodded, "I owe you an apology, Alex. I never should have left you guys in California. I can't even tell you how many times I was sure I would never see you again. I'm happy we're together again but I just can't wrap my head around what's happening here. I mean, how did these guys take over the town so easily? Are they really going to hold our families and everyone else hostage for the long term? I just can't see that lasting. How are they going to feed everyone and keep them under control? I just don't get it!"

Alex turned her head and looked through the forest in the direction of the fields. "We don't know a whole lot of what's going on but we know they are using a lot of them for labour to work the farms. Hopefully by the end of the day we will have a better idea of what's happening. We're only guessing that they are planting Quinn's, Josh's, and our farms because they're the biggest in the area. We need information and that's what we're doing today." Alex faced Emily again and a hard look came over her face before continuing. "Listen, we need to be prepared for what we might see. We have no idea what kind of condition our families are in or how they are being treated. We have to stay strong and not do anything stupid. No matter what we see, we can't go charging in. We have to stay hidden if we have any chance of making a plan to free everyone. No matter what we see today, we have to stay quiet and just watch. Can you do that?"

Emily swallowed hard before nodding. "Do you really think we can save everyone, Alex?"

It took a minute before she answered and when she did her voice was quiet and full of concern.

"I don't know but I won't give up until we do or I die." Alex made a fist and looked at it thoughtfully before standing up. "Come on, let's go."

Emily quickly closed the backpack and slung it over her shoulder before grabbing her rifle and following her best friend down the ladder. They made quick time through the rest of the trees and when they were close enough to see the first field, they started to take cover and crawled to the edge of the trees.

Quinn's grandparents' farm was straight ahead of them and Alex could see the roof of the barn in the distance. There wasn't anyone near them so they rose and skirted the field, staying just in the tree line for cover. Just as they were coming inline to the barn, a shot rang out and both girls flattened to the ground. Alex met Emily's wide-eyed stare and gave a quick shake of her head. She didn't think they'd been spotted and the shot had come from the vicinity of the barn which was still a full field ahead of them. They stayed down a few minutes just in case and two more shots rang out.

"What are they shooting at?" hissed Emily in frustration.

Alex scanned the closest trees around them and reached for the backpack that Emily had dropped. She pulled out a pair of binoculars and pointed at a thick tree and motioned at herself and then up. Emily nodded in agreement but her heart was pounding in fear for her friend.

Alex stayed in a crouch as she went to the tree she had pointed at. Putting the tree between herself and the barn, she put the binoculars strap over her head and tucked the glasses in to her shirt so they wouldn't bang against the trunk of the tree as she climbed. Scanning the branches above her, she found the one she wanted, and using a knot on the trunk, launched herself up to the lowest branch. Alex had been climbing trees all her life and with her gymnastic conditioning it was no effort to haul herself from branch to branch until she was twenty feet up. She freed the glasses and brought them to her eyes and focused them on the barnyard. It took a few moments for her brain to catch up with her eyes and with all the uncertainty and fear she felt over the well-being of her family, the scene through the glasses made her stomach lurch from horror. The blood she was seeing was from three steers that were being butchered, not slaughtered. Alex watched as groups of four men hauled ropes attached to the carcasses to get them hanging. Once she got her emotions under control she started to scan each face she could make out and her heart leapt with joy at the broad shoulders she recognized. When the man turned in her direction she felt tears well up at the face of Harry Dennison, Quinn's grandfather.

She had to lower the glasses for a minute to clear her eyes. That man meant so much to her. For as long as she could remember he had been in her life. He was the kindest man and so many times she would sit on his fence and chatter away a mile a minute and he would just patiently listen to all she had to say. She reached up and tugged at one of her red gold curls, something he had done ever since she had wandered over to his fence the first time when she was five. Alex wiped away her tears and looked down at Emily's upturned face. She gave a reassuring smile and a thumb up which eased her anxious expression before training the glasses back towards the farm.

There were a lot of people working around the farm. There was a huge area around the barnyard that had been cleared and tilled and at this distance, Alex guessed that they had planted garden crops. It was also easy to tell the guards from the workers because they all held some sort of long gun. After scanning the entire area she was surprised to only count six guards. Taking another look around she tried not to focus on the workers' faces but it was hard not to look at each one to see if there was anyone else she recognized. After another careful count, she came up with over sixty townspeople on the farm and still only six guards. After thinking about that for a minute, she realized that they didn't need more guards while the families of all these people were being held hostage. No one would cause any trouble if their children were being threatened.

Alex looked out into the far fields to see if there were any others working further out but didn't see anyone. Deciding that she had seen all she needed to on this first scout, she couldn't help but bring the glasses back to the barnyard to have one more look at Quinn's grandfather before moving on. Her breath caught in a gasp when she focused on him and he seemed to be looking right at her. She knew that he couldn't see her from so far away so she just watched him for a minute and was confused when he slowly brought his hand up and pointed in her direction and then ran his finger over his throat in a cutting motion. What was he doing? Why would he make that gesture? She scanned the men around him to see if anyone had noticed what he was doing but the two guards were watching the men wrestle with the beef carcasses. When she trained the glasses back on Mr. Dennison, he was still looking in her direction and with his body blocking the guard's sight was using his hand in a shooing manner.

Alex lowered the glasses and leaned back against the tree in confusion. There was no way he could see her from that distance so what was the meaning of his actions. Without using the glasses she looked back out at the fields and had to shade her eyes from the sun's bright glare. She squinted into the distance before her eyes widened in realization. Before the thought had fully formed in her head she was wiggling down the tree. She dropped down beside a surprised Emily and grabbed her backpack and quickly shouldered it.

"We have to go! Mr. Dennison saw me. I don't think anyone else did but I don't think we should take that chance."

Emily looked at her doubtfully. "Alex, there is no way anyone could have seen you from that far, calm down!"

Alex shook her head and held up the binoculars. "Not me, these! The sun is shining right at us. Every time I moved the glasses around, there would have been a flash. If I hadn't had some of the tree for cover, it would have been as clear as a signal flash! What a stupid mistake!"

Emily grabbed the glasses from her and ran to the edge of the tree line. She carefully shaded them with one hand and looked towards the farm. After a few anxious minutes, she turned and came back.

"Okay, no one is headed in this direction but I agree we should move on just in case. What did you see up there? Did you see anyone we know?"

Alex took the glasses back from her and packed them away. She knew what Emily really wanted to know. "Our families weren't there. The only person I really recognized was Quinn's grandpa. It looks like there are around sixty people working the farm and six guards with rifles and shotguns." She threw her pack back on and started to walk back the way they had come. "Let's get deeper in and then head north. We can cross the road where it dips down and then head to my place. After that we will have to leave the trees and cross over one of our fields to get to your land. That will be the hardest part as the grass isn't very high yet so we won't have much cover."

The two girls made their way deeper into the forest on silent feet. They had traveled these woods so many times while playing, exploring and hunting throughout their childhood that they felt confident and moved quickly. They moved deeper into the woods before turning north and travelling parallel to Quinn's homestead. Alex was nervous about what they would find at her home. She had been so happy to see Mr. Dennison alive and well that her heart was filled with hope at the prospect of seeing her father.

The girls caught sight of the road through the trees so they slowed down and approached it cautiously. They stayed inside the tree line following the road until they came to a section that dipped down. They could cross there without being seen from a distance. After waiting a few minutes and listening for any sounds of people nearby, they dashed across and were quickly concealed in the trees again. Alex and Emily continued through the forest without speaking. Both of them were consumed with both worry and hope for what they were about to see. It had been so long since they had seen their families and now they were close to getting some answers.

As the girls moved through the trees, they started to hear a faint rhythmic noise. At first they couldn't make out what was causing the sounds, but the further they walked, the louder it got. They finally came to a stop. Emily pulled out a water bottle and took a drink before handing it to Alex.

"Wood chopping," Emily said.

Alex cocked her head to the side and listened. She could hear many axes banging against wood and the sound of a tree cracking and then falling came to her. She nodded her head at Emily.

"You're right. They're cutting down trees. We are going to have to get around them. Hopefully they aren't too deep in and they are cutting close to the field." She scanned the trees around them and pointed out a large solid one.

"Your turn! See if you can get high enough to see how far away they are."

Emily strode over to the tree Alex had pointed out and studied the branches before dropping her pack.

"Give me a lift, please."

Alex laced her hands together and Emily placed her boot into them. With a heave, Alex helped her friend up so that she could easily reach the lowest branch. Emily might not have Alex's gymnast flexibility but she had spent just as much time climbing trees. She made her way from branch to branch until Alex lost sight of her behind the leaves. Alex kept her eyes and ears on the forest around them. She didn't want to take a chance that someone would stumble upon them. Her anxiety was at an all-time high before Emily finally jumped down from the tree.

Emily picked a scrap of bark that had slivered into her palm while she told Alex what she had seen.

"I couldn't see any people from up there but I could see the trees they are working on swaying around. They're about two hundred yards ahead and closer to the tree line at the field. If we stay on this heading, we should have about thirty to forty feet between us and them," she finished and then blew on her burning, scraped palm.

Alex turned away from her friend and looked in the direction of the chopping. She thought about what to do for a minute and then turned back.

"Okay, we'll keep our distance but it'd be great if we could get close enough to hear anyone talking. We can go up into the trees to get a better look at who's down there but I don't like the idea of being up a tree if we are spotted. I'd rather be on the ground if we are seen so we can run if we need to. What do you think?"

Emily grinned, "Super sneaky ninja mode?"

Alex smothered a laugh. "Yup, super sneaky ninja mode!"

Both girls were smiling at the many memories of sneaking up on the boys while they camped out. It was a game the group had played many times. They had to sneak up to the other's campsite and pull some kind of prank before getting away undetected. When they had left for the school trip, Alex and Emily had been in the lead by two pranks. It was no contest for the girls with Josh always giving away the boys. As hard as he tried, he just couldn't move silently through the woods and the girls always caught them before they could pull their prank.

Alex pulled the dark cap she was wearing down further on her head. She made sure all of her hair was tucked up under it and checked Emily's as well. Emily's white blond and her bright red hair would be like a beacon if they left their heads uncovered. Satisfied that they were ready, the two girls headed towards the woodcutting area. They walked slowly and watched where they put their feet. They might be seen but they wouldn't be heard. As they came closer to their objective, the noise of many axes filled the forest and they slowed even more. Using trees and bushes for cover, they inched their way closer to where the people were working.

Alex could see movement ahead so she crouched down and stayed low. Her heart was thundering in her ears and she paused for a minute to take some calming breaths before moving ahead. She settled behind a large tree and leaned slightly to the side so that only one of her eyes could see what was happening ahead of her. A man she didn't recognize was standing twenty feet in front of her in profile. He had a rifle slung over his shoulder and his arms were crossed with a scowl on his face. He was watching something further away so Alex eased back behind the tree and leaned the other way to get a view of what he was watching.

Two men she vaguely recognized from town were working on a downed tree. Most of the branches had been cut off and they were tying rope around it. Once they had the rope secured they both took an end and started to pull it towards the tree line and out into the field. The guard turned and followed them without looking in Alex's direction.

Alex pulled back behind the tree and looked back at where Emily was hiding. Her friend made eye contact and motioned for them to move on. Keeping low to the ground, Alex moved back and the two girls slinked further into the woods. Emily was in the lead and after a few minutes she used her hand behind her back to motion Alex to a stop. After a slight pause, Emily motioned Alex forward and down. They both settled behind a large bush and they carefully parted some of its lower branches to see what was ahead.

Both girls recognized the lone man working on stripping the branches of a downed tree. It was Dr. Mack. He had moved into their town five years ago and he had treated both girls over the years. Alex scanned all around the area he was working but couldn't see anyone else around. She turned her head until she was looking at Emily and raised her eyebrows and made a talking motion and pointed back at the doctor. Emily frowned and shrugged. With this many people in the woods, it would be hard to get a good look at the farm, and they needed the information. Alex knew they had to be careful not to give themselves away but the desire to find out what was happening to her family outweighed her fear. Her heart was thundering in her chest so she took a few deep breaths and parted the branches again. Taking another good look around the area and finding it still clear, she called his name in a low voice.

Dr. Mack paused in mid-chop and his body froze for a second before he followed through with his cut. When he pulled his axe back, he casually looked around and then whispered,

"Who's there?" while keeping his eyes on the tree he was stripping.

Alex was quick to respond. "Don't whisper, it carries further. Just talk in a low voice." At his nod, she went on. "It's Alex Andrews and Emily Mather. How many guards are there?"

Dr. Mack took another swing at the tree before responding. "There are six guards but you can't do anything. Our families are being held hostage."

Alex was quick to reassure him. "We know the situation. We're just scouting and getting info to make a plan. Doctor...where is my father? Is he okay?"

The doctor chopped at the tree a few more times with a frown on his face. Alex could tell he didn't want to answer her and she went cold all over. Was she about to find out that her father was dead? Just when her anxiety reached its peak, he looked around the area again and finally answered.

"He's in the barn. He had an accident a few days ago and cut his leg very badly. I've tried to keep it clean but it has gotten infected. This group of guards are real hard cases and they won't give me any medical supplies to treat it. I'm hoping when they rotate out that the next group will help me. Unfortunately that won't be until Sunday when we go into town. I'm sorry, Alex. I don't know if he will make it that long."

Alex was starting to panic and she was about to hit the doctor with a barrage of questions when Emily grabbed her arm and motioned for silence. It was only then that Alex heard the whistling. Someone was coming. The girls flattened themselves even further down on the ground and Alex prayed the doctor wouldn't speak and give them away. Seconds later, she saw another guard step up to the fallen tree. As he looked over the doctor's progress, Alex studied him. He was tall and rough looking. His hair and beard was long and greasy but he looked well fed with a gut hanging over his belt. Standing beside the doctor, it dawned on Alex how thin and tired the doctor looked. These bastards weren't feeding the workers very well based on the doctor's appearance.

"You better speed up, Doc. You don't make your quota, you don't eat!" the guard said menacingly.

Dr. Mack kept chopping at the tree as he answered. "We would be able to work faster if you guys would sharpen these axes. The blades are so dull it takes a lot longer to cut through every branch." His tone was bland as if he didn't want to antagonise the guard.

With a shrug of indifference, the guard started to walk away. He called over his shoulder as he went, "Life gave you lemons. Make some lemonade…if you want your supper!" He let out a howl of laughter.

Dr. Mack stood staring after the guard until he was out of sight before turning and looking in the direction that Alex and Emily were hiding in.

"Are you still there?" he called softly.

Alex lost all her caution and stood up. She couldn't help her father until she had more information.

"How many days is it until Sunday?" she asked him. They had lost track of the days of the week long ago.

"Today is Wednesday," he said, looking into her eyes sadly.

Alex shook her head. If her father's leg was infected, he couldn't wait that long for medicine. It could turn gangrenous and then he would die. She wasn't going to let that happen.

"Where do you all sleep at night and how many people are being kept here?"

"They lock us into the barn at night and there are sixty of us. There are another ten who stay in the house with the guards. They are working for them for more food."

Emily's breath caught at that. The idea that some of her neighbours would collaborate with these animals against their own people made her sick. She popped up beside Alex and asked her own question.

"Do you know what other farms are being used? How do the guards rotate?"

He gave her a sad smile and nodded. "Your family farm is being used as well as two others. The Dennison farm and another but I don't know who the owners are. On Sunday's they walk us into town and we get to see our families. They are being held at the school and we only get to talk to them through the fence. After a very brief visit, the guards switch out and we walk back for another week of slave labour." He took a quick look around to make sure it was still clear before saying, "You girls need to get out of here. If they catch you..." he trailed off with a frown.

Alex had to push down the fury at all that he had told them and focus on what she could do right now.

"I can get you medicine and first aid supplies. Will you be working here for the rest of the day?"

He shook his head. "No, this is the last tree for me. After it gets pulled out of here, we will all be back in the yard chopping, splitting and stacking for the rest of the day. I'm sorry, Alex, but your dad wouldn't want you to risk getting caught for him. You have to stay away."

"Yeah, well, that's not going to happen! What time do you get locked in and is there a guard in the yard at night?" she asked, in a 'don't argue with me' tone.

"We work until it gets dark and then they lock us in with whatever they are feeding us for supper. I'm pretty sure they don't put out a guard at night but it's not worth taking a chance, Alex. You have no idea what kind of animals these men are."

"Trust me, Doc. I know exactly what they are. I need someone to make sure that the hay elevator door is unlatched. I will be back tonight after dark with everything you need. Be safe and tell my father I'm coming!"

Chapter Four

The girls moved away from the area, quickly putting distance between them and the men working in the woods before circling around and heading north again. Even though they had the information that they needed, they still wanted to take a look at Emily's home. It was close to noon so they settled down for a break in a clearing and they pulled out the lunch they had brought with them. Alex picked at the peanut butter and jam bun sandwich as she thought about her dad. After five minutes of silence, Emily broke into her gloomy thoughts.

"I'm sorry about your dad. If it was my father, I would do the same thing but we really need to talk about this. If you get caught, it might blow our chances of freeing everyone," she said softly.

"I won't get caught, just like you wouldn't get caught if you had to sneak around your place. This is our home turf, Em. Nobody knows our farms like we do. I could probably sneak into my house without getting caught!" At Emily's startled expression, Alex laughed. "Don't worry. I won't be going anywhere near the house. The barn is between the house and the fields so they won't have a line of sight on me. Then I will climb the hay bale elevator up into the loft and I'm in. Piece of cake!"

Emily was still frowning. "We'll see what everyone else thinks when we get back to base, I guess."

Alex's face took on a set expression. "I'm not going back to base. We'll scout out your place and then I need to go and get some supplies for Dr. Mack. You shouldn't have any problems getting back to the bikes. Just leave mine and I will be back later."

"What!? Alex, there is no way you are doing this by yourself! Forget it! Besides, where are you going to get the medicine your dad needs? You have to come back with me and then we will all make a plan!"

"Not going to happen. Don't bother fighting me on this, Em. I'm going alone. If for some unlikely reason I get caught, then I need the rest of you guys to keep working on a plan to free us. I'm not risking anyone else. It's my dad who needs help, so I'm the one who's going to do it. Besides, I really don't think I'll get caught."

Emily threw up her hands and growled in frustration. She knew how stubborn her best friend was and there was no use in arguing with her right now. She also knew that there were many hours before it got dark and she could be back with help before Alex made her move.

"So where do you plan on getting these supplies? Last time I checked the Shoppers Drug Mart was closed."

Alex smiled with relief that Emily wasn't going to keep arguing with her. She also felt bad about the half lie she was about to tell but she had made a promise and she was going to keep it.

"Mrs. Moore's house is only one more road over and just to the west. She told me she has some supplies stashed away if we needed them. After we check on your place, we'll come back here and split up. I'll get what I need and then make my way back here and hang out in the trees until dark. I don't plan on staying very long in the barn so I should make it back to base by ten o'clock."

Emily looked away and took another bite from her lunch. She understood where Alex was coming from. If it was her father who was hurt, she would do whatever it took to help him, but she liked to think that she would ask her friends for help. It was just like Alex to not want to put her friends in jeopardy. Emily finished her sandwich and took a long drink from her water bottle before changing the subject.

"So where do you think the best place to cross the field is?"

Alex packed her water bottle away before answering. "I've been thinking about that. Do you remember last year when we played paint ball wars? We used that shallow gully along the fence in the north pasture to get to the tree line. We will still have to crouch down and the bottom will probably still be wet but I think that's the best bet to get across unseen. After that, it gets tricky. It's all open pasture on your land except for that one copse of trees on the northwest side. We will have no cover at all as we cross the fields. What do you think?"

Emily looked in the direction of her land and thought about it. "We won't get a very good look from those trees. They are too far away. If we go south at your property line, we can come up behind the cattle shelter and use that for cover. It's not much but with the glasses, we can get a good look at the yard and outbuildings. We're just going to have to play it by ear. We don't know where they are working and we will have to watch our backs in case anyone is on the east side of your place. Let's just see what's what when we get closer."

Alex stood up and slung her pack over her back before adjusting the sling on her rifle so that it wouldn't get in the way while she was moving. They set off through the trees heading back towards the distant fields. Alex thought about the farms that they knew were being used. If she had to guess she would say that Josh's family farm was the fourth one being occupied. Quinn's and her farms were mainly crop farms with small amounts of livestock. Emily's farm had some crops but they had a lot of poultry and horses. It made sense that Josh's family farm would be the fourth because they had the most cattle in the area. They also had a sizable herd of pigs. If the bad guys hadn't moved in and taken over, those four farms with the other smaller spreads wouldn't have had a problem supporting the local population. There was no shortage of food in this area and it made Alex furious that the workers were half-starved.

It didn't take the girls long to see the break in the trees ahead of them and Alex shimmied up a tree to look ahead and get their bearings. They had moved far enough away from her barnyard that there was no one in sight. Searching the fields ahead of her, she finally saw that they had to backtrack a bit to get to the area they wanted to cross over. She made her way back down the tree and landed lightly on her feet. Her muscles felt good and limber from all the walking they had done and it was a nice feeling after spending so long without exercise.

"We overshot it so let's move up to the tree line and head back a bit," she explained to Emily.

They stayed just inside the trees and moved more cautiously until they saw the fence and gully ahead of them. Alex passed the binoculars to Emily and she scanned the area around where they would be leaving the trees. She passed them back to Alex with a nod and after they were put away, they stepped out into the field. The girls ran in a low crouch until they reached the gully and scrambled down into it. Alex's boots landed in a few inches of water that was left from the melt-off. Keeping their heads down, the girls headed east. They traveled silently with their ears alert for any other human sounds for fifteen minutes. Their backs started to ache from their hunched over postures so when they came to a fairly dry area, they stopped to rest.

Emily leaned against the steep side of the gully and carefully used the glasses to scan back towards Alex's place before turning them towards her own. While she did that, Alex dropped to her knees and went into a few yoga maneuvers to stretch away the tension in her back. When Emily was satisfied that they were clear, she turned away and had to slap her hand over her mouth to muffle her bark of laughter. Alex had her hands and feet on the ground with her butt sticking straight up into the air. Emily watched her complete the move with amusement sparkling in her eyes.

When Alex straightened up and saw Emily's expression she raised her eyebrows.

"What's so funny?"

Emily's grin widened. "Just thinking about last year. If Josh had come across you like that you would have green neon paint splattered all over your butt and a heck of a bruise. You wouldn't have been able to sit for days!" she laughed.

Alex started to giggle. "That bugger always tried for a butt shot! He didn't think it was so funny when we ambushed him from behind and coated his rear with pink neon. I thought Quinn was going to pee himself laughing when Josh limped out of the trees and turned around to show him!"

They were lost in the happy memory when a distant gunshot cut off their laughter and had them dropping flat to the ground. All joy left them when the hard reality came crashing back that it wouldn't be paint balls headed their way if they got caught.

After a tense minute with no more shots, Alex grabbed the glasses and peaked over the edge. The shot had come from far away and when she couldn't see anyone in range they moved on. They stayed silent for the rest of the way and when they came to the end of the gully they cautiously looked around before leaving its protection. This was the scariest part so far. They were surrounded by open fields with no cover except for calf-high grass. There was no choice but to move out into the open so they just ran until they came to the fence that separated the two properties.

Diving down next to it, the two friends just lay still, and let their heartbeats slow down as they got their breath back. Before long they were moving again as they followed the fence line. It was ten minutes later that Emily came to a stop and motioned for Alex to hand over the glasses. Straight ahead of them in the distance was the outline of the wooden cattle shelter. It was on a slight rise and from the other side of it they would be able to see down into Emily's barnyard. There was nothing between them and it, but they had no way of knowing what was on the other side. Emily looked at Alex who just shrugged so she turned the glasses back towards the west and was happy to see only empty fields.

Stowing the glasses again, Alex held down the lowest barbed wire running through the fence and Emily climbed through. She did the same for Alex and then they both made the mad dash towards the cattle shelter. Just as they were about to top the rise, they both threw themselves down to the ground and struggled to catch their breaths. Using her elbows to pull herself forward, Alex advanced until she could peek over the top and see if anyone was in sight. She couldn't see anyone around but her sight was blocked by the shelter so she closed her eyes and just listened. After a few minutes of only hearing the soft sound of the breeze rustling the grass and background insect noises, she waved the all clear to Emily and they

moved the rest of the way up and over to the back side
of the shelter. Going separate ways, the girls each took
a side and edged around the corners. A quick wave
from Emily and they moved around the shelters sides
towards the front. They stayed crouched down as they
met in the middle and moved into the shelter and
behind a dry water trough.

They rested for a minute and gulped down more
water before Alex handed the binoculars back to Emily
and she moved over to the wall and edged out to the
opening again. Emily spent a good five minutes staring
through the glasses as she took in the changes to her
home. At one point Alex saw her tense up but then her
shoulders relaxed. Alex was getting anxious to know
what was happening when Emily finally let out a
breath and lowered the glasses. She came over and sat
down next to Alex without saying a word. Alex studied
her best friend's face but she could find no clue to
what Emily had saw.

"What did you see? Did you see your dad?" she
finally asked.

Emily passed the binoculars to Alex and nodded
her head. "Yeah, he's there. He seems fine."

Alex waited for more but Emily just looked down
at her raised knees.

"What is it? What's wrong, Em?" Alex asked in
confusion.

"Nothing…I don't know. It's just…after all this
time away, everything we've been through to make it
home, it's not supposed to feel this way. It's
like…making it home was a race and the prize was
supposed to be mom and dad waiting here to make it
all better. Now WE have to make it all better. Arggg, I
don't know how to explain it! I just feel let down for
some reason."

Alex turned and put her arm around her friend's shoulders. "I get it. I really do. It does feel wrong. Our parents have always been there to take care of us and fix any major problems we've had but now we have to fix our problems instead. I guess this means we're grownups now." She huffed out her own frustrated breath. "I always thought it would be fun. You know? We would get our own place and a cute car and go out to restaurants and pubs and we would have so much fun. Now we have this and it's not fun at all!"

Emily leaned her head against Alex's and they stayed there for a while thinking about all the things that might have been if the world had stayed the same. Both girls were too practical to indulge in a pity party for long so after a few minutes Emily sat up and nudged Alex.

"Come on. Take a look and see if you can figure out what they're doing down there. I could see where they did a lot of planting but right now it looks like almost all of them are building something and I have no idea what it is."

Alex nodded and whipped a stray tear from her cheek before standing and taking her own long look at the activity going on around Emily's home. After quickly scanning the nearby fields and noting where the planting had been done, she focused in on the construction site. There were piles of lumber stacked to the side and a long, one story building was being framed in. It was hard to tell from this distance but using the barn for scale, she guessed it was around a hundred feet long. The framing that had gone up so far suggested that there would be multiple rooms. Looking away from the construction, she focused on the people in the yard and quickly spotted six guards. They were easy to spot as they were the only ones with weapons and they were also all sitting or standing around not working. A smile came to her face when she spotted Emily's dad carrying some two by fours across the yard. He looked strong and healthy but it was hard to tell from this distance. Seeing all she was going to, she dropped the glasses and turned back to her friend.

"I don't know what they are going to use that for. I can't see these guys caring about more housing for our people so maybe it's for food storage. They will need somewhere to put the harvest when it comes in. What I do know is that it won't matter. We are going to take these bastards out and I think I have an idea on how to do that!"

Emily smiled at Alex's fierce expression. "Well, pull up a piece of trough and fill me in!"

Alex sat down and thought for a minute before explaining. "Okay, so far it looks like there are six guards at each farm. We will have to see what Josh and David find out but let's just say I'm right. Cooper was told that there are around sixty bad guys in the gang so we have twenty four on the farms and we took out seven on the highway leaving twenty nine or thirty still in town. That's still way too many for us to take on so we have to get that number down. Follow me so far?" At Emily's nod, she continued. "Okay, so Dr. Mack said the guards rotate out on Sunday when they take everyone to town. What if on Saturday night we take out the guards on each farm? There's only six at each place so we should be able to manage that many with all of us. Now here's the tricky part. We need to make it look like those guards all took off. When no one shows up in town on Sunday, they will either send a couple guys out to find out what's going on or they will send the whole guard rotation. Either way works for us. We fill our people in on the plan and split up all the guns we have between the farms. Our people will need to stay locked in the barns and pretend that they were locked in and left there when the first group of guards took off. If only a few guys come out to check on them, then they play possum until the six man team comes out. Once the full team is back in place then our people spring the trap and take them out. So let's do the math. The first group of twenty four guards, the second group of twenty four guards and the seven we took out on the high-way leaving how many in town?"

Emily was nodding. "Five."

"That's right, five bad guys against the eight of us and all the freed people from the farms." Alex finished.

Emily thought about it for a minute before responding, "Okay. Here's the flip side of that. They managed to take over our whole town and have kept control for just over a month so whoever is in charge is not stupid. He might believe that something happened to his guys on the road or that they took off but is he going to believe that twenty-four of his men just took off? Doubtful. Next, say they *are* idiots and the first part of the plan works perfectly. Now there are five very desperate bad guys in town with most of the women and children as hostages. What's to stop them from killing them one by one until the town surrenders again?"

Alex scowled in frustration. "Damn it! We need to know what's happening in town. Hopefully Cooper and Dara will get some good info and we will be able to figure that out. All I can come up with is infiltration." At Emily's confused expression, she explained, "While everything is going down out on the farms, the eight of us are in town. The girls find a way to get into the school with weapons and the boys take up positions around the school. We take out whoever is in the school from the inside and then lock it down to keep the women and kids safe. The boys take out anyone outside of the school. Anyway, it's just a rough idea for now. Run it by the others when you get back to base and we will see what the others found out today."

Emily frowned at the reminder that Alex was going on a solo mission. She realized that it was getting late in the afternoon and if she wanted to get to base and back before Alex made her move then they'd have to get a move on. She stood up and shouldered her pack.

"Come on. Let's get out of here. We still have to make it back across the fields, and if you're going to get to Mrs. Moore's house and then back by dark, we have to move it."

"You're right, let's take a scan around in all directions before we move out," Alex agreed.

They scanned all the directions around them and made the quick dash back down the rise. Once they were through the fence they backtracked the way they had come and were quickly back in the half-cover of the gully. The trip back seemed to take a fraction of the time now that they weren't anxious about what they would discover. They made the last dash to the tree line without seeing anyone and both of the girls found comfort being back in the cool, dim protection of the forest. When they made it back to the clearing where they had lunch, they dropped their packs and drank from their water bottles. A quick snack of beef jerky was had in silence. Alex's thoughts were back on her father and the medicine he desperately needed. Emily was plotting the fastest route back to the bikes. She didn't have to backtrack the way they had come this morning so she would make better time getting back. She was dreading Quinn and Josh's reaction when they found out what her stubborn best friend had planned.

The girls stood and embraced each other before pulling apart. Emily yanked Alex's cap further down on her head.

"Keep your head down and be safe!"

Alex nodded and held up her hand for a slap. "Cake!"

Emily slapped her palm. "Pie!"

And with a cheeky grin, they both said, "Don't split!"

Once again, the best friends split up in this dangerous, new world.

Chapter Five

Alex took a deep breath of the cool moist air in the trees. This was her favorite time of year in the forest. Everything was new and green, but the mosquito population hadn't exploded into a flying menace yet. She moved quickly and with confidence down the familiar trail. She knew the exact route to take that would get her closest to Mrs. Moore's house without having to leave the trees. She wondered if anyone had looted her teacher's home and felt a pang of sadness at not knowing her fate. She smiled to herself as she pictured the formidable older woman. If anyone could survive in the city, it would be Mrs. Moore. It was hard not to dwell on the state of the world and how nothing would ever be the same, but she pushed those thoughts away and tried to stay focused on her own little piece of the world and what needed to be done. She was relieved to know her father was alive but her mind kept going to her mom and what she was going through. How hard it must be for the people trapped in town, not knowing what was happening to their husbands. She prayed that the men holding them weren't abusing the women and the rage that flashed through her at the thought had her quickening her pace.

As Alex approached the next road she had to cross, she slowed down and listened for any sounds that would alert her to danger. Hearing only the birds in the trees, she stepped out of the trees and looked both ways. As soon as she saw that it was clear, she dashed out and jumped over the ditch and across the road and into the trees on the other side. She wasn't as familiar with this area, but she knew that there was one house between her and Mrs. Moore's property. Alex didn't want to approach the houses from the front so she planned on circling around behind them and coming from the rear. That way she could stay in the trees and watch the house before getting closer.

It only took a few minutes for her to see the first house through the trees and she paused to listen for any noises. Hearing nothing, she continued on until she saw the outline of a shed behind Mrs. Moore's home. Keeping the shed between her and the house, she moved closer to the tree line and the backyard. Kneeling behind a bush, she scanned the ground behind the shed looking for the cellar doors that Mrs. Moore had told her about. The grass had grown a bit wild and it was hard for Alex to see what she was looking for from her location, so she moved parallel to the yard and took a good long look at the house. Her heart sank when she saw the back door standing open. Someone had been to the house and that meant there was a good chance that all of the supplies had been stolen. She just had to hope that no one had discovered the cellar hidden somewhere behind the shed. Movement caught her eye and she almost laughed when a squirrel scampered out the open door and rose up on its hind legs on the back step. It chittered away for a few seconds before turning and going back into the house. That was all Alex needed to see to know that there were no humans in the house.

Taking one more look around the yard and trees that surrounded the yard, she rose and walked across the grass to the back door. She climbed the steps and pushed the door open even farther. It was dim, but she could see a mudroom and an open door that led further into the house. On soft feet, she made her way through the mudroom and peeked around the corner into a ransacked kitchen. Hearing no sounds from within, she stepped into the room. All of the cabinet doors were hanging open and most of the drawers had been pulled out and their contents dumped on the floor. There were empty shelves in some of the cabinets and Alex guessed that food had once been stored in them.

Angry squirrel chatter filled the room making Alex turn towards an archway that led to the dining living room combo. She shooed the critter away and inspected each room on the main floor. The place was a mess and no care had been taken when whoever had searched the place went through it. She had to stop herself from cleaning up the disaster. If anyone came back here it had to remain as they left it.

Once she had cleared the main floor, she took her flashlight from her pack, and opened the basement door. Alex knew that Mrs. Moore's supplies would be gone but she felt the need to make certain before she went for the teacher's backup supplies. She shined her light down the unfinished basement steps and was happy to see that it wasn't completely black down there. Alex ignored the shudder that ran down her back as countless teen horror movies came to mind. Her head screamed out the classic "don't go down into the dark basement" line as she stepped down onto the creaky stairs. By the time she made it to the bottom, her heart was pounding and she gave a little laugh at herself when the scariest thing she saw was spilled laundry soap dusting the floor.

The two small windows let enough light in that she didn't really need her flashlight, but she kept it clutched in her hand anyway. There wasn't a lot to see. In one corner was a pair of laundry machines and a small utility shelf with all of its cleaning supplies thrown on the floor. Turning away from it she panned her light on the area furthest from the windows and saw a small sitting area. There was a table with a knocked over sewing machine and some bolts of fabric and that was it. She was disappointed that there was nothing that she could use and turned away to leave but something in the back of her mind made her stop and turn back. She looked over the small area again and frowned. Why was it so small? The laundry and sewing area didn't even make up half the size of what a basement should be. Mrs. Moore had told her that the basement was full of supplies so where would they have been stored? Other than the utility shelves, the walls were bare. Her teacher wouldn't have just piled her things on the floor so where was all the shelving or storage containers? Alex scanned the walls more closely looking for another door but came up empty. Three of the walls were bare concrete. The only finished wall was behind the sewing table and it was wallpapered with an ugly pattern. That one wall was so out of place from the rest of the unfinished room that she couldn't stop looking at it. She finally walked over to it and started to run her hand along it. As soon as she felt the slight bump in the wall, the answer clicked in her head and a grin broke out across her face.

Alex stuffed the flashlight into her pocket and used both hands to feel the wall. It took only seconds for her to find the second bump and she gave the area between the bumps a fast push. She laughed out loud when the section popped out a few inches and a door was revealed. She shook her head in admiration of her crafty teacher. Someone as prepared as Mrs. Moore wouldn't have left her valuable supplies laying around for anyone to find.

She pulled the door open and pointed her flashlight inside. The room was completely blacked out, but her light's beam showed her five rows of floor to ceiling shelving. As she moved further into the room she could see metal cabinets attached to the walls. Alex opened the first cabinet to her right and shone her light at its contents. Five large battery operated lanterns took up the main shelf so she grabbed one without much hope that it would work. Finding flashlights that worked had been hit or miss for her group and she didn't really think that the pulse had spared these lanterns. Flicking the switch on, she almost dropped it when bright light pulsed out of it.

Alex was giddy with delight as she tried all five of the lanterns and the room slowly lit up. She sighed sadly that such a small thing as light could give her joy in this new world. Stowing her now unnecessary flashlight, she explored the rest of the cabinet. The top shelf had two rows of four walkie talkies sitting in bases. She smiled ruefully at them and though about how handy they would be now that cell phones were obsolete. She still unconsciously reached for hers sometimes to dash off a quick text. Alex reached up and pulled one down. It was one thing for a simple lantern to survive the pulse but she knew that the hand held had much more complicated and delicate wiring. Ghosts of the old world had her thumb pushing the dial up on the side and she stared in wonder at the soft green glow as the power button came on and the digital readout that told her it was set to channel one.

After being stunned by what she held in her hand she lunged forward and flipped the switch on all of the handhelds. When eight green eyes glowed back at her, she closed her eyes and sent prayers and blessings to Mrs. Moore. Alex didn't know how they had survived the pulse. Maybe it was because they were stored underground or in a metal cabinet, but she really didn't care. She was so happy she wanted to dance on the spot. Being able to communicate would make things so much easier in their mission to free their town.

After carefully shutting off all the walkie talkies, she took a lantern and started to take an inventory of everything that was in the room. She kept shaking her head at the sheer amount of goods piled up on the shelves. Rack after rack was filled with dried and canned food. One whole unit held nothing but candles and Sterno fuel cans. When she came to a section that was filled with medical and first aid supplies she huffed out a happy breath. There were many boxes of different sizes of bandages and shallow boxes filled with blister packs of pills. Alex was worried that she wouldn't know what type of pills her farther would need until she opened one of the pill boxes and saw a four by four inch index card that listed the different ailments that the pills would be used for.

It didn't take long for her to locate the medicine and painkillers her father would need and she took only enough to treat him and left the rest on the shelf. Mrs. Moore's words on the importance of these supplies had stayed firmly in her head. As much as she felt like a kid on a shopping spree, she knew that these supplies had to be left here for a greater emergency and she had high hopes that Mrs. Moore would someday return home and need them.

Looking over the rest of the medical supplies, Alex found small trays that had sterilized suture kits and scalpels. She grabbed two and added them to the pills and bandages she had already put into her backpack. With her father's needs taken care of and time to kill before dark, Alex wandered through the room and marveled at everything Mrs. Moore had accumulated. There were so many things that Alex had taken for granted in the old world, from big bottles of different vitamins to boxes of chocolate bars. There was a section that held nothing but different types of clothing and winter gear and even a selection of boots in different sizes. The huge amount of storage in this room had Alex wondering what was in the storm cellar. How many years had it taken her teacher to accumulate all of this and where had she gotten the funds to purchase it all? She didn't know, but was grateful for the medicine that would help her father.

Thinking of her Dad made Alex check the time on her old windup watch. It was just after five o'clock and being surrounded by all this food made Alex's belly rumble. Deciding to stay here until closer to dark, she closed the door to the rest of the basement and found a desk to put her things on. She didn't think it would be too bad to help herself to one meal from Mrs. Moore's stock as all she had left in her pack was water and some beef jerky. She grabbed one of the small fuel cans and a cooking frame to go over it and selected a can of chunky beef stew for her meal. The stew warmed in its can as she did some more exploring. Seeing all the food on the shelves made her think of Dr. Mack's weight loss

The guards obviously weren't feeding the workers much and she wished she could find a way to get food to them but her pack would only carry so much and she wanted to take the handheld radios with her. Boxed cases of power bars caught her attention and she pulled one from the shelf, testing the weight. The box contained fifteen bars and hardly weighed anything. She might not be able to feed her neighbours a real meal but she could at least give them this.

Alex emptied her backpack and sorted out what she would need to keep. The handgun would go in a holster on her belt and she would wear the extra sweat shirt she had brought. She repacked the hand held radios and medical supplies and then filled her bag with seventy power bars. Thrown in loose the bars didn't take up more than half her bag so she started to hunt through the shelves for something else she could take the half-starved townspeople. Alex found what she was looking for in cellophane wrapped sesame snaps. They were small but high in sugar and protein.

She dumped them in on top of the power bars, added the binoculars and closed her pack. She lifted it to test the weight and was happy to feel it only slightly heavier than before she had started.

The smell of her dinner filled the room and she found a spoon and dug in. It was far from gourmet, but the warmth filled her and satisfied her after a long day of walking. She cleaned up her small meal as best as she could and topped up her water bottle from one of the many jugs stored in the room. Alex couldn't stop thinking of her dad. The guard had told Dr. Mack that he wouldn't eat if he didn't make a quota but she hadn't seen her father working at all. Doing another quick search of the room, she found a small camping pot and filled it with water before placing it on the stove frame to boil. There were four stainless steel thermoses on the camping gear shelf so she grabbed one and carried it over to the desk. Once the water was boiling she added six bouillon cubes and made beef broth before pouring the mixture into the thermos and adding it to her pack.

Alex checked her watch and saw that she still had an hour before she wanted to head back to her farm so she searched through the desk and found sheet after sheet of inventory on the supplies in the room. Alex spent the next thirty minutes leafing through the papers and contemplating what would happen in the night to come. She was getting more anxious by the minute and finally gave up waiting and moved around the room, shutting down the lanterns she had lit.

When she left the room and secured the door, she took another look around the rest of the basement. Her footprints stood out clearly in the spilled laundry soap so she picked up the half-filled box and started to toss soap flakes over her prints as she walked backwards to the stairs. As she stepped onto the lowest step she tossed the empty box into the corner and continued up the stairs. Before she left the house, she found the key under the sink to the cellar and stopped in the mudroom where there were blue boxes for recycling. She selected an empty glass jar with a lid and peeked out the backdoor to scan the yard. Finding it clear, she strode across the overgrown grass to the shed and started to search the ground for the cellar doors. Alex spent ten frustrating minutes walking back and forth looking for the doors. She wouldn't have found them at all if she hadn't heard the slight creak of boards when she stepped on one area of grass. Dropping to her knees, she felt around the area and found a small depression that her fingers followed. Hooking her fingers under it she heaved up and almost laughed when she saw the flat square board that was covered in soil and grass. She lifted it enough to see the actual doors and padlock before dropping it back down. There was no need to go into the cellar at this time and she didn't want to disturb the hiding place any more than she already had.

After making sure the grass covering the doors looked natural, she turned and went into the trees. Directly behind the shed at the tree line was a large evergreen. She went to it and searched the forest floor for a thick stick. She found what she was looking for and took it to the evergreen. Parting the lower branches, she got on her hands and knees and crawled between them. Behind the long draping branches was a large opening around the trunk. These were Alex's favorite types of trees and they made the best hiding spots. She and Emily had outwitted the boys in many games by slipping into the openings before popping out to ambush them.

Using the stick, she dug a hole between two of the thick roots and took the key for the cellar out of her pocket and put it into the jar. Making sure the lid was on tight she put the jar into the hole and refilled it. Now if anything happened to Mrs. Moore's house she would have access to the cellar. Satisfied that her work at the teacher's home was done, she crawled back out between the branches and settled her pack more firmly onto her back. After tightening the straps and repositioning her rifle, she slowly started to backtrack around the property and headed deeper into the woods. She definitely could feel the extra weight she had added to her pack but was determined to get the small amount of nourishment to her neighbours.

The sun was slowly setting as she crossed the road and made her way through the trees that lined her property. The light filtering through the trees became dimmer and she placed her feet with care until she came to the area the men had been cutting trees in. There were no longer any chopping sounds and the forest was empty. Alex circled around the cleared area and made her way to a large tree closer to the field. She dropped her pack in relief before removing her binoculars. She studied the branches before jumping to the lowest branch and hauling herself up. When she was high enough to see the field between her and the barn she settled into a crook against the trunk and started to scan the barnyard. With the sun behind her she didn't have to worry about it reflecting off the glass and giving her position away like earlier in the day.

A line of smoke coming from the yard made her heart clench before she realized that it was a cooking fire. A table had been set up and two large pots were resting on it. The workers were lined up holding bowls and as each one stepped up, they received a single ladleful of whatever they were eating for supper. After each man left the line they made their way to the barn and disappeared inside.

Alex thought about the long day of labour her neighbours had just put in and the small amount of food they had been rewarded with. It was not something that could go on. Their bodies would get weaker and weaker before breaking down and she wondered what the guards would do once that happened. She felt immense sorrow when she realized that this was bound to happen soon, after living like this for a month. She clenched her jaw in anger. They needed to free their people and it had to happen soon.

She stayed in the tree for the next forty five minutes and watched as the yard emptied of men. The food table was taken away after some of the workers received a second helping. Alex narrowed her eyes in anger as she watched these men take their extra food into her home. She kept a close count on the guards as they moved around the yard. Long shadows filled the barnyard as the sun sank behind the distant mountains and all the guards except one headed into the house. The lone remaining guard entered the barn but stepped out within seconds and closed the big double doors. He used a large beam to secure them by dropping it into brackets on the outside. After he had joined his friends in the house, Alex concentrated her glasses on the hayloft door and the hay elevator that ran from there to the ground. The hayloft door had been secured from the outside with a board set in brackets like the main door. As darkness settled over the land she concentrated her sight on her house. The only light showed from a few windows and she watched for another hour to see if any guards came out to patrol the yard. Each time the door opened and spilled light out her shoulders tensed but after the fifth guard came out and did his bathroom business she hoped they were done for the night.

After almost two hours in the tree, Alex's body was stiff and sore and she slowly made her way down to the forest floor. She stretched out her back and legs and looked down at her heavy pack. She had to climb the hay elevator and she had to do it as silently as possible. Shaking her head at the weight, she knew she would have to leave some of her gear behind. Just as she picked up her pack, sounds of branches cracking came to her from the west. Her heart started to pound and sheen of sweat developed all over her body. Looking around frantically she ran to the closest evergreen and pushed her pack between the branches before crawling into its interior opening. She tried to calm her ragged breathing but her body was filled with adrenaline.

Frustration filled her because she was so close to helping her father and she prayed that it was an animal traveling through the trees. As the sounds moved closer to her, she closed her eyes and concentrated on it, waiting for what would happen next. After spending years playing in the woods, Alex soon realized the sounds coming toward her were not being made by an animal.

Chapter Six

Cooper and Dara had made good time getting to town. They weren't as familiar with the trails and pathways that ran through the trees on the west side of town but after studying the hand drawn maps their friends had made for them, they were confident they could make it undetected. There was a roadblock on the main highway two miles from town that they had to circle around but they stayed far enough in the trees that they weren't seen. The community center, school and most of the residential areas were on the south side of town and they would have to cross the main highway at some point to get to those areas. Cooper led the way, as he was more familiar with the business area and back alleys than Dara.

When they came to the tree line, there was a green space that ran between it and a few industrial buildings. They took their time and watched the area for signs of movement but saw nothing. After twenty minutes of watching, they decided that the area wasn't being used so they dashed across the green space and through a parking lot. Using the building for cover, they again waited and watched the highway. Directly across from them was an access road that led into a new residential development, under construction when the pulse hit. They planned on using that area to travel deeper into the south side of town and hoped it was abandoned. Still not seeing anyone around, the two crossed over the main road and moved quickly into the construction area. They cautiously walked past half-finished homes that would quite probably never be lived in. The silence was eerie in a place that should be alive with men hammering and sawing.

The construction site was protected by a chainlink perimeter fence that separated it from the next subdivision. They followed it around until they could see a paved pathway on the other side. They had packed light for the day of scouting with only one small pack with food, water and a notebook and pens. They both carried handguns but had left their rifles back at base. If they were caught, they didn't want to have to explain where they had gotten the powerful rifles. They also knew that they would have to climb fences and that'd be hard with the rifles. Both of them had brought heavy gloves to protect their hands while climbing fences.

Cooper studied the houses on the other side of the fence and saw only empty windows staring back at him. He turned back to face Dara.

"After we go over this fence, we can follow the path down the backside of these houses. It'll cut between two of them and we can follow it further in to town. I know that most of these pathways lead to Fairways Park and the school and community center both back on to it. If we can get into the school, I know how to get onto the roof and we'll be able to see all around from there."

When she just nodded, he stuck his boot into an opening in the fence and hoisted himself up. Chainlink fencing was easy to climb except for the very top. Sometimes it had a bar running along the top but this fence only had the exposed links sheared off creating many sharp points that needed to be straddled and climbed over. The support posts were set close enough together that there wasn't a lot of sway in the fence but Dara braced against it to make it even steadier. When he made it over to the other side, he did the same for her and they both headed down the pathway.

Walking through the abandoned neighbourhoods was surreal. They kept to cover as much as they could and watched carefully before crossing into the open but they never saw anyone. They took a break in a small playground and seeing the empty play structure with its lonely swings swaying in the breeze made Dara sad. She was desperate to know what had happened to her little brother and prayed she would she would get some idea of his fate today. Sipping from the water bottle she studied Cooper, who was gazing off in the distance. He had been very quiet since he had talked to his father's friend at the roadblock. He helped out around the base camp and offered his opinions on their plans, but there was an emptiness to him. The spark from his eyes was gone and he hadn't laughed or joked since he found out that his father had been killed.

"Did you want to go to your house? Maybe you could find some of your stuff to take back or get some family pictures or something?" she asked, trying to bring him out of his funk.

Cooper didn't look at her. He just let out a bitter laugh and shook his head. "I don't want anything from that place. The only reason I would go there now is to burn it down!"

Dara frowned in concern. There was so much anger and bitterness in his tone.

"I'm sorry about your dad, Cooper."

He finally turned to look at her with shocked confusion. "What? Why would *you* be sorry? I'm the one who is sorry! My father did all of this! He's the reason all of your families are suffering!" His sharp blue eyes were filled with anguish and a sheen of tears before he turned away.

Dara couldn't believe they had missed it. All this time, Cooper had been blaming himself for what his father had done. He kept his distance because he thought they all blamed him. She had to try and fix this and make him understand that he wasn't to blame.

Dara rubbed at her face and tried to come up with the words that would reach this sad boy.

"Did you know that my mom is a drunk? She doesn't just drink. She guzzles the stuff until she's passed out. She spends more time in an alcoholic coma than she does awake. She's been doing it for years. My little brother and I have been taking care of ourselves for so long. I hope he's okay but I wasn't here when the pulse hit so he might be…dead. That's my fault." Her voice broke on the word dead.

Dara felt guilt for not being here to protect her brother but she knew it wasn't her fault. She had done her best to take care of him, but it was her parents that had failed him. She was trying to make Cooper understand that he wasn't to blame for what his father had done and the incredulous look he gave her made her hope he would.

Cooper kneeled down in front of Dara and took her hands. "That's not your fault! You didn't make your mom drink. It was her and your dad's job to take care of you and your brother. This is their fault, not yours!"

Dara lifted her head and met Cooper's eyes. She raised her eyebrows and her expression said "SEE?" Cooper was confused by her response and asked "What?"

Dara tilted her head and asked him softly, "How come it's not my fault what my mom did, but it is your fault what your father did?"

His eyes darkened and he tried to pull away from their joined hands. Dara wouldn't let him go and told him, "This is not your fault! Your father sold out this town. He was a very bad man and that has nothing to do with you! I don't blame you for any of what he did and no one else does either. Let this poison go, Cooper."

His expression softened and he looked hopeful for a split second before the sound of a motor starting up came from close by. They dropped hands and quickly scrambled around to the opposite side of the structure and crouched under the slide. The motor sounds were getting louder and it was clear that it would pass close to them, so they flattened out on the sand and kept their heads down. The vehicle traveled past them on the street and as it drew away, Cooper risked raising his head enough to get a look. The car was an old antique convertible that had been restored and he could see two people in it. When the car turned the corner and traveled parallel to the small park they were hiding in, he got a better look at it occupants. There was a woman driving and it looked like a teenage girl in the passenger seat.

Cooper stared at it in confusion until it was out of sight and then helped Dara to her feet.

"That was really weird. I don't know who they are, but there was a woman and girl in that car," he told her.

Dara's face showed surprise. "Really? Maybe there are some people that are free!"

Cooper looked thoughtful. "I don't know. If there were people free we would be seeing more of them around. Let's get going. The only way we are going to figure out what's happening here is if we go look."

Dara nodded, and after taking a good look around, they left the playground and entered the pathway system that ran between two houses that faced the playground park. Moving closer and closer to Fairways Park, they still didn't see any movement. When they came to a street that was only two blocks from their school, Dara turned down an alley and motioned for Cooper to follow.

"Where are we going?" he asked.

"My house is just down here. I want to go in and grab a few things."

Jogging down the alley, they stopped at the fifth yard down and slowly peeked over the gate, looking to see if anyone was around. It seemed just as abandoned as the other houses they had passed, so they entered through the gate and made their way to the back door. Dara tried not to look at Jake's toys scattered all around the backyard. She didn't really need anything from the house. She was hoping there might be a clue inside to tell her what had happened to him. When they got to the door they looked through the window but couldn't see anything. Instinctively, Dara reached for her pocket to get her house keys. She almost laughed out loud when she remembered that they were in her suitcase in California. Cooper gave her an inquiring look but she just waved it away before trying the knob. She wasn't surprised when it turned freely in her hand and the door popped open. Her mother wasn't very good about remembering to lock the doors.

They stepped into the dim house and stood still listening for any movement. They both felt that the house was empty and when Dara went further in, Cooper closed the door behind him. The kitchen had been cleaned out and most of the cabinet doors had been left hanging open. She walked further into the house and expected to see her mom passed out on the couch like always. Dara felt nothing when she walked around it and saw that it was empty. The coffee table in front of the couch was piled with empty wine bottles and an overflowing ashtray. Turning away with disgust, Dara left the room and went down the hall to her brother's bedroom. She knew right away that some of his things were missing but she didn't know if he had taken them on his sleepover when she left for her school trip or if it was later, after the pulse. She huffed out a frustrated breath and left his room. She went to her own bedroom and grabbed some clothes and personal items before joining Cooper back in the living room.

Cooper turned around when he heard her come in and held something out to her. It was a piece of paper, but it was too dim in the room to read it. They went into the kitchen and Dara opened the blinds over the window above the sink to let some more light into the room. When she finished reading the words in the note, she wordlessly handed it to Cooper and closed her eyes in relief. Tears streamed down her face as she said a silent prayer of thanks to Josh's parents for taking care of her brother. She might not know what happened to him after the gang took over but she knew that Josh's parents would have done everything they could to protect him.

Cooper gave her a one-armed hug before pulling back. "Let's get to the school and see what's happening at the community center. You never know, we might even get a glimpse of your brother!"

Dara gave him a grateful smile. "Do you want to go to the high school or the middle school?"

Prairie Springs had three schools in town. The high school and middle school were separated by the community center making it easy for the students to walk across the parking lot to use the center's pool. The third school was an elementary school for the younger grades and it was located further away.

Cooper thought about it for a minute and came back with, "High school. I know how to get on the roof if we can get in. The back playing fields all connect so we can circle around to the middle school if we need too. We will just have to see what we find when we get there. We don't even know if they are still being held at the center so let's play it by ear for now."

Dara nodded and took a final look around the house she used to live in. Even if they freed the town, she didn't think she would ever live here again.

"Let's get out of here. There's nothing here for me anymore." She walked out and closed the door firmly behind her. They stayed in the alleyways as they made their way closer to their school. This was Dara's area of town and she knew the best way to approach the back playing fields. She had traveled this path every day to and from school for the past few years. When they came to the last street of houses that butted up against Fairways Park, Dara pointed out the pathway that ran between two of them.

"If we take that path it leads to the main park and the schools are on the other side," she told Cooper. "There are a few sections that have good tree cover we can use."

"Good idea. I wish we had binoculars but hopefully we can get close enough to see what we need," he said.

They ran down the street and turned on to the pathway between houses. They had only gone halfway when Dara skidded to a halt. She turned and waved Cooper back the way they had come. He didn't waste any time asking why, just turned and followed her back to the street. Dara cut across the lawn of one of the houses and paused at the gate to the houses backyard. She turned to Cooper with a concerned look.

"There's a chainlink fence blocking the path. It wasn't there the last time I walked this way to school, so we need to get a look at what's happening in the park before we try and go into it."

Cooper looked around the street and then up at the house they were standing beside. "Okay, let's see if we can get inside this house. It's a two-storey so we should be able to get a good view of the park from the back upper floor windows. Stay here. I'm going to check the front door to see if it's locked."

Dara nodded and Cooper ran to the front door and put his ear against it. He stayed there for a minute before trying the doorknob. Just like Dara's house it was unlocked. Briefly wondering if all the doors in town were unlocked, he waved Dara over and they slipped into the empty house.

Both teens had not had very loving homes and it had made them wonder about how other people lived, but being in a stranger's house was just plain weird. It felt really wrong to just walk through someone else's house and Dara had the urge to take her boots off and leave them by the front door. Pushing the feeling away, she pointed out the stairs to Cooper and they headed up. They picked a child's bedroom that faced the park and each took a side and carefully pulled back the pink lace curtains until they could see out over the backyard and into the park.

The extreme changes to the park left them both speechless. The whole area had been transformed and Dara couldn't even imagine how many people it had taken to change it so much. There were no longer any trees in the park. They had all been cut down. She could see a few stumps sticking up from the ground but everything else was gone. The next big difference was all the grass had been removed and in its place was row after row of tilled soil. There was some new growth in the rows and she guessed they were some kind of garden crops. With all the trees gone, Dara had a clear view of the back of the schools and community center. She could also see the new fence went all the way around the park and schools. Inside of the fence were people. She could clearly make out women on their knees working along the rows and further away there were groups behind the school. She pulled away from the window and settled on the child's bed to think.

Cooper paced the room as they both thought about what they had just seen. He finally settled down beside her and took a deep breath.

"That wasn't what I expected at all! I thought they would all be in one building. It looked like they were using both of the schools and the community center. I could only count six guards in the Fairways but there has to be a lot more. We're too far away to see how many are around the buildings." He was silent for a minute and when Dara didn't respond he asked her, "What do we do now?"

Dara stood up and went back to the window. She stayed there for a few minutes before turning away and looking at him. "We need info, we have to make contact."

Cooper stared at her in disbelief. "What...No! We all agreed not to make any contact today. It's too risky! If we tip our hand and the gang finds out, we will have no chance at all of freeing this town."

Dara shook her head. "And if we don't find out what's going on here and how many guards there are, we won't be able to make a plan. I know it's a risk but we don't have a choice!"

Cooper leaned over and rested his elbows on his knees. He stared at the carpet between his feet. Dara stayed silent and let him work through it. She knew he would agree but she didn't want to push him so she turned back to the window and watched the people closest to them and the fence. She had just picked out the most likely candidates when Cooper stood up and joined her at the window.

He looked down at the people doing gardening and asked her, "How are we going to talk to those people?"

Dara pointed out two girls working together further down the fence line. "See those two? If we count the backyards along the fence we can figure out what house is closest to them. We go into the yard and call out to them to come closer and ask them what we need to know. With any luck they won't do something to give us away. As long as the guards stay over where they are, it should be safe enough. If they don't work, there is a woman working close to the fence in the other direction. We do the same thing with her. It's the best I can come up with right now. I don't want to go back to base without some serious info to make a plan. The longer we sneak around like this, the more chances we have of getting caught."

Cooper took a deep breath and nodded. "Okay, but we have to be really careful. What color is the house closest to those girls?"

Dara turned back to the window and studied the backyard closest to the two girls that were weeding one of the planted rows. She couldn't see the house from this angle but she could count how many yards were between the house they were in and the one they wanted to be in.

"I can't tell what color it is but its six houses down. The nearest guard is half the park away and he looks like he is sleeping on the bench he is sitting on. I think one of us should go into the house if it's unlocked and keep watch from a window and the other should try and get their attention through the fence."

Cooper went to the window and took one more look at the park before turning away and walking to the door. They left the house after scanning the street to make sure it was still clear and made their way down the block to the house they had targeted. Again, they found the front door unlocked and they came to the conclusion that the whole town had been searched by the gang. This house was a bi-level so they made their way to the highest level and found a room with a rear facing window. Nothing had changed in the park in the few minutes since they had last looked except that the two girls had moved to a row closer to the fence.

Cooper looked around the room and went to the closet. He opened the door and looked up before grabbing a nearby chair and placing it just inside the closet door. He climbed up on to the chair and used the built-in shelves to climb higher. Pushing on the ceiling, he raised up a panel that revealed the access opening to the attic. Cooper stuck his head through the opening and looked around before quickly climbing down. He faced Dara and gave her a serious look.

"If for any reason I get caught, I want you to climb up into the attic and hide while I lead them away. Just climb the shelves and put the hatch back in place. Wait until dark and then slip out and get back to base."

Dara opened her mouth to argue but Cooper held up his hand to stop her. "Listen to me Dara, I have no one left. You have Jake so I want you to promise me that you will hide and let me lead them away from you." He could see that she wanted to protest but the thought of her little brother made her slowly nod her head in agreement.

They went to the window and looked out at the two girls again. Cooper checked that the guards were still in the same position before opening the window an inch and telling Dara, "Keep a close watch on the guards. If it looks like any of them are headed this way, try and let me know but don't give yourself away." Dara nodded and gave Cooper a tight hug before stepping back.

"Be careful. Don't tell them too much, just try and get numbers and locations for now."

Cooper nodded briskly and turned and walked out of the room. He made his way down to the front door and after a quick look to make sure the street was still empty, he slipped out and crossed the front lawn to the gate to the backyard. He winced at the creak of hinges when he opened it but didn't think it was loud enough to carry into the park. He closed it as quietly as he could and followed the wooden fence to the back of the yard. The panels in the fence had a half inch of space between them and he stopped a couple of times to look through the openings. When he was even with the two girls he took a deep breath and clenched his fists before calling to them in a low voice. The girls didn't respond. His body thrumming with tension, he called louder.

The girl closest to him froze as she was reaching down to pull a weed, slowly lifted her head and glanced around. When she was looking in his direction, Cooper called out again and he saw her flinch. She looked to be around the same age as Cooper and he thought he had seen her in the halls of school, but he wasn't sure from this distance. He watched as she said something to the other girl and then turned to look back where the nearest guard was sitting on a bench. They both stood up and picked up the garbage bags they were filling with weeds before moving a few rows closer to the fence. When they settled back down and started to pull weeds again he was going to call out but saw one of the girls looking right at the fence he was hiding behind. She used her body to shield her hand that was in a stop gesture so he settled back to wait.

Cooper's nerves were strung tight and he had to fight himself not to fidget. He turned and looked up at the window that Dara was watching from and he saw her hand appear with a thumb's up so he relaxed a fraction. The wait was agonizing, feeling like hours as the two girls slowly made their way closer. When they finally were at the last row, all that separated them was the paved walkway and a few feet of grass that ran up to the other side of the fence. Cooper looked up at Dara one more time and she gave him the all clear. Before he could start talking, one of the girls beat him to it.

"Who's there?" she asked, in a low nervous tone.

Cooper tried to keep his voice steady as he replied, "We're friends. We're trying to make a plan to free everyone but we need information."

The two girls shared a quick look with each other before continuing to pull up weeds. Cooper was confused by their response and was going to say more when the other girl spoke up.

"How do we know you aren't trying to trick us? You could be one of the gang. We don't even know who you are."

Cooper was quick to try and reassure them, "No, I'm not with them! I think we went to high school together. My name is Cooper Morris. I'm a senior at Prairie Springs High."

He thought that would convince them but it had the opposite effect. Their faces changed to anger and hate and one of them spat out at him, "Get away from us, you scumbag! We aren't going to fall for your trap! You and your father are the reason we're in this mess. You're disgusting!" The last word was said in a snarl and both girls grabbed their bags and walked back the way they had come and settled back down to continue working.

Cooper was stunned by the venom in the girl's tone and fell back onto his butt. He just sat there feeling waves of shame wash over him because of all that his father had done. He couldn't even blame them for lumping him in with his father. The reputation he had allowed to develop painted him as a bad boy, petty criminal, so why would anyone trust him? He must have been lost in misery long enough for Dara to become worried because the next thing he knew, she was kneeling beside him and staring into his face with concern.

"What is it? What happened? Cooper, what did they say?!" He could hear the panic creeping into her voice and it knocked him out of his stupor.

"Whoa, it's okay, Dara! They didn't say anything. When I told them my name, they thought I was part of the gang and that I was trying to trick them. They won't tell us anything," he explained.

Dara looked at him in confusion. "I don't understand?"

Cooper hung his head and muttered, "My father."

Dara cursed softly, "Forget about them. We'll try someone else."

Cooper was shaking his head in defeat when a voice caused them both to freeze in panic.

"Is someone there?" They heard someone call from the other side of the fence.

The only thing that kept them from bolting was that the voice came from a female. Dara slowly turned her head and peered through one of the gaps in the fence. She saw the woman they had seen further down the field when they had been looking for someone to approach. The woman was pretending to pull weeds where the girls had been not that long ago and she kept stealing glances at the fence that Cooper and Dara were behind.

Dara pitched her voice low but loud enough to carry. "Yes, we're here! We're with a group that's trying to put a plan together to take back the town. We need information. Can you help us?"

The woman looked to be in her forties but it was hard for Dara to make out too many details through the small gap in the fence. The woman didn't even ask any questions. She just started to tell them the situation.

"The men are all out on farms. I don't know what it's like out there but we see them on Sundays and that's when the guards are rotated. There are just over sixty gang members holding the town. Over twenty are on the farms watching the men and the rest are in town. Most of the women and children are kept in the high school and there are ten guards that watch over us in the yard and the park. The rest of the gang are split up around town at road blocks. They sleep in a few of the nicer homes but most are in the hotel at night. They have a pleasure house where some of the women work. We are all locked in to the school at night and I don't know how many guards patrol. We're paralyzed to do anything because they punish our husbands if we cause any trouble and they punish the women if the men do anything. They have executed more than twenty men and women since they took over." She paused and glanced towards the bench the guard had been sitting on and froze when she saw it empty. In a desperate voice, she whispered "Go! Get out of here! Good luck!"

Dara was about to run away when she had a thought that made her turn back. "Don't let those girls tell anyone we were here. Don't tell anyone!"

When she saw the woman nod her head and make a go away gesture, she spun around and followed Cooper out of the yard.

They made their way in silence back through the town without stopping until they crossed the main highway and had circled around the roadblock through the trees. Once they finally felt safe, Dara stopped Cooper with a hand on his arm.

"Cooper, those girls are wrong. It's not your fault."

Cooper lifted his head and met her gaze with the saddest eyes. After a few seconds he dropped his head and continued walking. Dara rubbed her eyes at the injustice and followed him back to base.

Chapter Seven

Quinn finished the last turn on the jack to level out the small camper he and Lisa had brought back from the resort storage compound. As he stood up, he felt a deep ache in his thigh. The bullet wound had healed cleanly but he still had pain after a day of activity. Absently rubbing at the ache, he turned and smiled at Lisa. The girl was almost unrecognizable from the stuck up, shallow cheerleader he had shared the halls of high school with. They had left the campsite base to search the resort's many campers in its storage yard while everyone else had gone to scout the town and farms and they were the first ones back. Quinn had been on edge all day long not knowing what was happening to his friends. For probably the hundredth time that day, he glanced at the old wind-up watch that had replaced his useless digital one that had fried with all the rest of modern electronics when the pulse hit.

Lisa passed him, carrying another load of supplies that they had filled the camper with. They had decided early in the day to bring one of the campers back with them to make sleeping arrangements less cramped. Lisa had slowly driven the antique truck to the resort with Quinn walking ahead to watch and listen for any traffic on the two roads they had to cross to get there. It was slow going, but with the encounter they had had the day before they were being extra cautious.

Once they had made it to the storage compound, Quinn had used a pry bar to open storage compartments under the trailers and some of them had laundry chutes that Lisa could squeeze through to enter the main living areas and unlock the doors. They had to choose trailers without slide outs as they had no power to open the slides and get access to the cupboards and pantries. Quinn had been surprised at how many people left dry goods in their campers over the winter and they had brought back enough food to last them for a few weeks if they needed it, especially if they had pancakes every day. Almost every camper they had checked had a box of just add water pancake mix in it.

Lisa had surprised him throughout the day by taking the initiative on doing what needed to be done. She searched for, and hauled, supplies without complaint and hadn't blinked an eye at squeezing into dirty storage compartments to gain access through the laundry chutes. She had some angry looking scrapes on her arms but she barely gave them a glance. She had definitely changed and Quinn was pleasantly surprised.

They worked together to unload the camper of all the supplies they had gathered and make up the beds for the coming night. They had brought back more sleeping bags and pillows as well as two solar showers they had found. Once they had the camper ready for occupancy, they went to work on rigging up the showers so the sun would have a chance to warm the water up. Lisa held up tarps while Quinn used scavenged rope to make privacy screens. They were both looking forward to even a quick shower later in the day. Anything would be better than the wash cloth wipe down they had been using for so long.

With the final knot tied, Quinn looked at his watch for what seemed like the thousandth time. Living life without any means of communication was a huge adjustment. The uncertainty of what was happening with his friends was wearing away at him and he looked around for something else to occupy his worried mind.

He grabbed the small hatchet they had and started to stack up branches to cut for their fire. The only campfires they had were at night. To keep the smoke from giving away their location, they had dug down and piled rocks in a low wall to shield the flames. Quinn finished cutting down the supply of wood they had on hand, so he checked on Lisa who was organising their supplies, before ranging out to gather more branches. He had only gone twenty feet into the surrounding trees when he heard the sound of tires on the gravel road approaching their base. There was no sound of engines so he knew whoever it was had to be on a bike, but he still crouched down and moved quickly back towards the campers. He had just made it to the back side of the new camper they had brought back when he heard Josh's voice blurt out, "Whoa!"

Quinn moved quickly around to the front to see what was going on. What he saw made him smile and impressed him even more. Lisa was just lowering one of the assault rifles with a sheepish expression. Josh and David were straddling their bikes with their hands in the air. When Quinn gave a bark of laughter, Lisa lowered her eyes in embarrassment. Quinn saw Josh's scowl and quickly intervened.

"Good job, Lisa! You were more prepared than I was. We have to stay on guard. It could have been anyone who stumbled on to our site."

Josh's face changed to a thoughtful frown before he nodded. "He's right. Good reflexes Lisa, but I think we need to give you some instruction on that gun."

Lisa looked from Josh to the large rifle in her hands before asking, "Just point and shoot right?"

Josh gave her his cheeky grin while nodding his head. "Yup, that's about it, but first you have to take the safety off!"

David and Josh parked their bikes and dropped their packs while Quinn showed Lisa how to arm the rifle properly. They would have to spend some time with her, Emily and David on how to use the powerful guns, but Quinn was more interested in what news the two boys had brought back.

All four of them gathered around the picnic table and spread out the hand drawn map. Josh and David leaned over it and started to put X's through the properties they had scouted out. Josh circled his family's farm and leaned back.

"We did a wide circle north and then east to come up from behind our areas. There are a lot of empty houses out there. All the small acreages and hobby ranches have been cleared out so we stashed the bikes and just walked through the fields to stay off the roads. We checked David's place first. It's completely bare." He showed them the route they had taken on the map.

David's face was grim when he put his finger on the X that represented his family's small farm.

"We didn't have a lot of stock but they took it all as well as all the feed from the barn. The house and cellar had been stripped of all food as well. I managed to grab some of my stuff but there was no sign of what happened to my mom and sister."

Josh put his hand on David's shoulder and gave it a squeeze before turning back to the map and running his finger through the area they had gone through. "All of these places had been stripped as well. I gotta tell you, Quinn, it was creepy! Even knowing that these guys had rounded everyone up, I thought we would come across somebody that was still free. Anyway, we went through the Stockton's fields because their place butts up against mine and there's that strip of trees along the property line. I figured they would give us some cover to get a good look at my place. Holy crappin' cow, was that place busy! I hardly even recognized the old place. There had to be at least a hundred men down there! A bunch of them were working on two different new buildings. They got a second barn framed up and being finished and some kind of long building that had lots of rooms framed in. I don't know if it will be for housing or storage, but it's big. The rest of the people were cutting meat. They had five hogs hanging and tables set up where feathers were flying. I can tell you that there's a lot more stock being kept there than when we left for Cali. If I had to guess, I'd say they're using my place for the main meat supermarket. It didn't look like they had done any planting in the fields, but it was so busy we stayed on the east side the whole time."

Josh stared at the map on the table and just shook his head at all the changes he had seen on his farm. Lisa broke the silence with the most important question.

"How many guards are there?"

Josh was still lost in thought so David answered her. "We counted eight. We stuck around and watched for over two hours, so unless some of them were in the house and didn't come out there were eight walking around. They all had shotguns or rifles but we were too far away to see if they had handguns too."

When he fell silent, Lisa leaned over and picked up the pencil and wrote the numbers on the map in the circle around Josh's home. Josh was thinking hard and he finally raised his head and looked at the others.

"We're going to have to go back. We need to know the schedule of the guards and what they do at night. Where do the workers sleep? How do the guards patrol? Stuff like that." He looked around the campsite and then back at Quinn. "Hopefully the other teams will find out more but we're going to need a few more days of watching to get a better idea to come up with a plan."

Quinn nodded thoughtfully before his expression changed to one of concern. "Did you see anyone you know?" He wanted to ask if Josh had seen his dad but was afraid of upsetting him if he hadn't.

Josh sniffed and looked away. Looking out into the trees he nodded. "Yeah, my dad was butchering a hog and I recognized some people from town and a few of my neighbours." When he turned back there was a steel rage shining from his usually happy eyes. "I saw Mr. Lock from the feed store. The only reason I recognized him is because he's the only man over six foot five that I know and he always wears that dumb blue floppy hat. You remember how big he is? Last time I saw him he had to be over three hundred and fifty pounds, now he's a bean pole. My dad used to have that big belly. Well, it's gone now. I think they are starving our people."

Quinn took a step back at the news. His mind flashed to his grandfather. The man was over six feet tall but he had always been lean and wiry without a lot of bulk. How would he survive at his age without food and having to labour all day? Quinn felt hopelessness flood through him and with a shake of his head he shoved it away. Alex and Emily would be back soon. They were scouting out his home before moving on to their own. Until they got back with news of his grandfather he wouldn't lose hope.

A flicker of movement in the trees had Quinn reaching for the handgun on his hip but he relaxed as he saw Dara and Cooper step into the campsite. He studied their faces for some sign of what they had seen in town but Dara's small smile of greeting told him nothing. Cooper looked like he was far away and wouldn't meet his eyes as he walked over and dumped his pack beside the picnic table. Josh grabbed Dara and gave her a fierce hug before draping his arm around her shoulders and looking relieved to have her back safely.

Quinn tried to get a read on what was going on with Cooper, but the guy just stood staring down at the map in silence, so he shot a questioning look at Dara. She just frowned and gave a small shake of her head before looking away. When she took in the new addition in the camp she brightened.

"Hey, that's great! Last night was a little cramped in the van. Now we can spread out a bit. Does it have enough bunks for all of us? As cozy as it was with us all in the van, I could do without the lovely boy aroma I woke to this morning!"

Josh gave her a nudge and grin. "How do you know that was from us guys? We all ate chilli for supper. It could have been from you girls!"

Dara laughed "After more than a month in close quarters with you? I could pick you out of a line up with my eyes closed just using my nose!"

Quinn saw Cooper's head come up and a brief smirk cross his face at their teasing, so Quinn asked him what they needed to know.

"Did you guys have any trouble getting through town?"

Cooper's face turned serious again. "No, we made it through with no problem at all but we couldn't get very close to the community center. We were going to use Fairways Park to come up to it from behind but they've clear cut all the trees out and fenced the whole thing. They've turned the whole park into one gigantic garden. We went in to a couple houses that back on to it and had a good view from the second floor windows. We could see that they're using both the community center and the high school to house people."

Quinn frowned at the information. "We'll have to find a way to get closer. We need more detailed information on how many guards are stationed there."

Dara shot a nervous look at Cooper before facing Quinn again. "Well, yes and no." She bit her lip and looked at Cooper again before blurting out, "We made contact," in a rush.

Everyone but Cooper looked at Dara in shock. Quinn overcame his first and stammered out, "What? We all agreed..."

Dara cut him off before he could finish his sentence.

"I know we agreed not to make contact with anyone from town but we couldn't get anywhere close to where they are being kept and there were some women working close to the fence so I just took a risk." She stared everyone down defiantly before continuing. "Look, we need information and that was the only way we were going to get it. I told her not to tell anyone so we should be fine."

Josh rubbed Dara's back in comfort and faced Quinn. "She's right. We need to know certain things and just watching isn't going to do it." He picked up the pencil and handed it to Cooper. "X out everything you know is empty and clear and circle what's occupied. Write in the number of guards where you can. When Emily and Alex get back, we'll add their info to the map and then decide what to do next."

As Cooper filled in the map, Dara explained what the woman had told them about the guards at the school and around town. She took the pencil from Cooper and drew in the one roadblock they knew of and marked in that there were four guards when they had last seen it. Beside the map, she wrote in the number sixty-five and circled it. Underneath that she made a minus sign and wrote the number seven. When Josh asked what the numbers were for, she straightened up and tapped the first one with the pencil.

"Everyone keeps saying over sixty guards so let's just call it sixty-five for now and we took out seven of them on the road. As we fill in the map, we can subtract the number of guards as we find out where they're posted until we know where they all are."

Quinn folded his arms and looked at the map before nodding at Dara and then Cooper. "You did good, guys. You were right to make contact. We now know a lot more than we did and we're getting closer to being able to make a plan."

Dara glanced quickly at Cooper and then away. Neither of them mentioned the first two girls he had approached and their reaction. They could only hope that the woman would make sure they kept their mouths shut.

Lisa led Dara to their new camper and showed her around before they both started to pull supplies out to make supper. Dara was laughing at the sheer amount of pancake mix they had scavenged when she heard Josh make a strangled yell. Both girls flew out the door and saw Emily with her hands on her knees panting to get her breath back. Dara looked around but didn't see Alex anywhere. She turned to Josh just in time to see him pull at his hair and mutter, "I'm going to kill her!"

Chapter Eight

Alex's heart was roaring in her ears and it felt so loud that she was sure that whoever was coming towards her hiding place would be able to hear it. Her brain was frantic with the thought that Dr. Mack had given her away and the guards were searching for her. Her rifle was too long to manoeuvre in the close confines of the tree, so she leaned it up against the trunk and pulled out her handgun, using her thumb to flip off the safety. She saw the outline of the person pass her tree through the thick needle encrusted branches and heard him grunt when the toe of his boot caught on a root. She let out the breath she didn't even know she was holding as the man passed by and stopped at the tree line and looked out into the barnyard.

Alex closed her eyes in frustration and flipped the safety back on as she holstered her gun. The grunt she had heard was all she needed to identify the person in front of her. Leaving her pack and rifle under the tree, she slipped soundlessly between the branches and crept up behind the person. Using her pointed finger she poked it into his back and whispered, "BANG! You are now covered in pink neon paint!"

Josh whirled around and grabbed her and pulled her into his arms. She was a little shocked by his intensity but hugged him back. She was just as surprised when he shoved her back and keeping a hold of her arms gave her a little shake.

"Alex, what the hell are you doing?!" he asked in a low, fierce voice.

She checked the yard over his shoulder but it was too dark to see anything so she pulled him back into the trees where she had hid her pack before answering. His accusatory tone had her temper rising. This was why she hadn't gone back with Emily to get the medical supplies from base. She hadn't wanted to fight with anyone about her decision to sneak into the barn where the men were being held. They had all agreed not to make contact with anyone on this first scouting mission and she had broken that earlier, when she approached Dr. Mack. She knew there would be an argument when her friends found out that she was going back.

She left Josh fuming as she crawled into the tree and retrieved her pack and rifle. When she emerged with her things and stood up he tried again.

"Alex..." he got out before she cut him off.

"No! I'm sorry Josh but I have to do this. My father is hurt and sick and if he doesn't get the medicine I have he could lose his leg or die! I know we said we wouldn't make contact but this is too important!"

"Alex, will you shut up for a minute?! I'm not here to stop you. I'm here to back you up! Of course you have to help your dad. Jeez, any of us would have done the same. I was just pissed that you tried to do it alone!"

Alex took a step back and looked away. She was feeling somewhat foolish that she hadn't given her friends more credit. Turning back to Josh, she gave him a sheepish shrug before grinning.

"So, let me get this straight, they sent the bull crashing through the china shop to come to my rescue? I mean, I could hear you coming from a mile away!"

Josh crossed his arms across his chest and gave her a baleful look. "Well, I was a little worried I wouldn't get here in time!" he said in frustration before looking around with concern. "Emily told us Dr. Mack said he didn't think they patrolled. Have you seen any guards?"

Alex shook her head. "No. They seem pretty confident with everyone locked in the barn. I guess no one would try anything with their families being held in town anyway."

Josh looked relieved that his loud approach hadn't given them away. "So, what's your plan?"

"Nothing too elaborate. I'll climb the hay elevator and go in through the hay loft opening, hand over the supplies, give my dad a hug and then get out. I won't be in sight of the house at all so I shouldn't have any problem."

Josh nodded in agreement. "Okay, I'm going to take cover behind the woodshed so I can see the barn and the house. If someone comes out while you are climbing, I'll give a bird call and if they come out while you are in the barn, I'll book it over and knock on the back wall. You should just try and hide inside if anything happens. We still want to keep the element of surprise if we can, so just shooting these guys is not in the cards unless we get desperate."

Alex kneeled down and opened her pack and started to pull her supplies out. "Yeah, about that? I have a better idea. Instead of you making a sound like a bird is being tortured, how about you just call me?" she said as she pulled out two of the handheld radios and handed him one.

Josh took the radio in surprise and flicked it to life. The soft green glow reflected off of his shocked face and his expression changed to delight.

"Right ON! Where did you get these? Never mind, tell me later!" he exclaimed as he flipped through the channels.

Alex just smiled as she turned her own radio on and set the channel before clipping it to her belt. She pulled the other six radios out of her pack to make it lighter. She didn't want to lose these precious resources if she was caught, so she put them under the same tree she had just hidden under, stowing her rifle as well. They could grab them on their way out if all went well. She shrugged her pack on and tightened the straps so it wouldn't move too much while she was climbing. Once she was ready, she gave Josh a thumb's up and turned to go. He grabbed her arm and pulled her back.

"Listen Alex, if it all goes to hell, just use the gun and get out of there. We will figure out a way to free our people no matter what, so don't let them take you. Okay?"

Alex's face was stone dead serious when she replied. "Don't worry, Josh. I'll kill them all if I have too."

Josh felt a shiver run down his back at her words and tone. They had been through so much in the last month and it had changed them all. Alex had always been a firecracker but now she was a little bit scary too. As he rushed to get in to position, he hoped that she wouldn't suffer long term damage by the things they had been forced to do. Sadly, he knew that in the coming days they might have to do much worse.

Alex stood at the edge of the trees and watched the dark outline of her friend dash across the open ground until he disappeared behind the shadow of the woodshed. She waited until she could just make out his arm waving her forward and took off like a shot, streaking the hundred yards to the back of the barn and stopping with her back against the old boards. She closed her eyes and listened to the night around her, she could make out a faint murmur from inside the barn, but the rest of the yard was silent.

Alex crept along the back wall of the barn, towards the slide-like hay elevator. She stopped directly under the hayloft door that was high up on the barn wall, then moved underneath the elevator and away from the barn until it was low enough to the ground that she had to go around to the side of it. Being as quiet as she could, she rolled over the lip on to the conveyer belt and froze. Still hearing only silence around her, she rose up onto all fours and started to climb. The metal creaked and flexed under her, sounding loud to her anxious ears, but she kept going. She was moving so slowly that it didn't seem like she was making any progress. Her mind flashed back to all the times she had run up this very elevator, using the round metal rollers like a fun balance beam. As she got closer to the barred loft door, she wondered if she'd ever be able to see her home without the taint of what these men had done to it.

Alex reached the top of the elevator and lifted the first two by four from the newly installed brackets. She placed it in front of her knees, balancing it across the metal rails of the elevator and repeated the move with the second. She would have to bring the boards in to the loft with her so they wouldn't fall to the ground, and then replace them when she left so the guards wouldn't know that anyone had been through it. Grasping the handle on the door she used slow, steady pressure to pull it open. The hinges on the door made a racket when opened too fast.

Alex froze in confusion and panic when the door only moved a fraction of an inch and would go no further. She tried again with the same result. Leaning her head against the cool metal of the door, her brain tried to process what to do next. She had told Dr. Mack to make sure the latch was unhooked. Why hadn't he done it? She stayed that way for a full minute wondering if she should abort her plan when a picture of her father in pain flashed through her mind. Alex gritted her teeth in anger. This door would not stand in her way of helping her dad.

Keeping one hand on the frame to keep her balance, she worked her other hand into her pocket and came out with a Swiss army knife. She got the longest blade open and leaned her upper body against the frame. Using one hand to move the door she slid the blade in her other hand into the thin opening. Alex pictured the latch on the other side in her mind and slid her blade until it made contact with the metal latch. Using gentle pressure, she pushed at the latch while wiggling the blade as much as she could. She didn't want to snap the blade off so she couldn't push too hard. Alex felt like she had been working on the latch for an hour and her fingers were starting to cramp. She felt tears of frustration build behind her eyes, and was about to give up when she felt the latch give.

She held her breath as she gripped the handle and once again tried to pull it open. A sob of relief almost escaped her when the door moved an inch. Moving the door a fraction of an inch at a time to keep it as quiet as possible she made a gap wide enough to slide the two boards through. Once they weren't in danger of falling to the ground, she inched the door open enough to squeeze through with her pack. Alex took a quick look around the loft and saw hay bales but no people. There was dim light coming from the bottom of the barn, but only silence greeted her. She had one panicked thought that the guards were down below, waiting for her to show herself, but she shook it away and trusted Josh to alert her to any danger. Even so, once the loft door was closed again, she unholstered her gun and crept on soft feet to the rail that overlooked the main floor of the barn.

Swallowing past a bone-dry throat, she leaned over the rail and peered down into the dim light of the main floor. This time a gasp did escape her. At least sixty men were packed together and all of them were staring back at her.

Vertigo struck her and she stepped back with dizziness. A low murmur came from the men below before a harsh voice shushed them. She could hear the men shuffling around below her before a quiet voice called her name. Alex's hands were slick with sweat as she clutched her gun and she stepped forward and looked down again. The men had made a small clearing, and in it stood Dr. Mack. His face was full of concern as he stared up at her.

"It's okay, Alex. It's just us in here," he called up quietly.

Alex scanned the men's faces anxiously. She recognized quite a few of them but didn't see her father.

"You didn't unlatch the door."

Dr. Mack shook his head, "I didn't have time to tell you earlier. There's no way to get up there. They took the ladder out. You'll have to drop down whatever you brought for your dad."

Alex was feeling very nervous with all the men watching her. She wanted to see her dad and she didn't understand why he hadn't shown himself yet. She had a panicked thought that he was dead and Dr. Mack just didn't want to tell her.

"Where is he?!" she demanded.

Dr. Mack held up his hands in a calming gesture at her tone, "He has a fever and he's sleeping. He doesn't even know you are here, Alex."

Before Alex could respond she saw someone push his way through the crowd to the doctor. She recognized her old gym teacher, Mr. Beck. The man was built like a bull and moved easily through the packed men as they made room for him. When he got to the doctor he launched into a tirade.

"What is this, Mack? Why didn't you tell us you had talked to this girl? Are you trying to get all of our families killed?" he asked, red-faced and outraged.

Alex wasn't going to come this far without seeing her father and she had to try and defuse the situation before Mr. Beck gave them away with his loud voice so she called out to them.

"I'm coming down!"

As she walked along the rail, Alex thought it might be a good thing that her dad wouldn't be able to see what she was about to do. This wouldn't be the first time that she had pulled this stunt, and if he ever caught her she knew he would kick her butt black and blue.

When she was even with one of the central support beams that ran across the barn, she threw her leg over the rail and climbed over until she was standing on the one foot wide surface. Her arms out for balance, she stepped away from the rail and calmly walked out over the heads of all the men looking up. Alex kept her eyes on the rope tied to the center of the beam and confidently walked to it. The end of the rope had been looped up and wrapped around the beam. The other end of the rope was attached to a thick metal pulley. Her father used the rope and pulley system to hang game carcasses for butchering. Balancing carefully, she lowered herself to one knee on the narrow beam, unwrapped the rope, and dropped it down to the floor. She checked that the thick knot on the other end was tight and secured against the pulley with a hard yank. Once she was sure it would hold, she dropped down onto her belly on the beam and slid off the side so only her upper body was still on the beam. Using her legs, she hooked the dangling rope between her feet and swung an arm over to grab the rope. After that it was a quick slide down to the floor using her feet as brakes to spare her hands from rope burn. She felt hands steady her and had the floor under her feet in no time.

Alex looked around and was intimidated by all the men looking back at her. She was at a loss for words and was starting to get nervous when Dr. Mack pushed through the crowd and took her arm.

"You do know that you aren't invincible, don't you? That was a crazy stunt, but now that you're down here let me take you to your father."

As Dr. Mack pulled her through the crowd she scanned faces and saw many gaunt and tired men. Many of them were smiling at her but there were also faces that were frowning and a few that even looked hostile. Dr. Mack was leading her towards the small office her dad kept at the end of the stalls. Now that she was here, and so close to seeing her dad after all this time, her anxiety was increasing. She had been through so much on their journey home, and, in a lot of ways, felt that she was a different person. Having killed men had changed and hardened her, and she was almost afraid to face her father. They were steps away from the door leading into the office when Alex felt her other arm being grabbed and she was spun away from Dr. Mack, coming turned face to face with her old gym teacher, Mr. Beck. His face was bright red, eyes angry, and his grip was painful on her arm.

"Alex Andrews, what do you think you are doing?! This game you're playing could get all of our families killed!" he spat out bitterly.

Alex tried to pull her arm away from him but he just tightened his grip and gave her a small shake so she looked in to his face and tried to calm him down.

"Mr. Beck, I know this isn't a game. I'm well aware of what is happening to our town and how careful we have to be. I'm not alone here and I have people watching the house. I'm here to see my father and give him the medicine I brought for him. I also have some things for the rest of you. If you will just let me go I will talk with you and everyone else after I've seen dad."

Mr. Beck didn't seem to care what she said and bullied on.

"Who are you with? How many? Is it the army? I want to talk to whoever is in charge!" he said loudly.

An intense anger filled Alex. Here she was, risking her life, partly to try and help this man, and all he was doing was hurting her. After all the care she took to get in here undetected and this loudmouth was going to have the guards opening the door at any minute. She tried one more time to free her arm and when he yanked on it even harder she snapped. Gritting her teeth against the pain and her anger, she used her free hand to pull her gun from its holster and drew it, pointing it straight at his head. Mr. Beck's eyes widened in shock but he didn't let go of her arm.

"How dare you point a gun at me? You little brat! You probably don't even know how to use it!" he said with contempt.

Alex was so sick of being patronized by adults. She hadn't felt like a kid in forever. The voice that came from her didn't sound like a child's. It was filled with cold hard steel.

"With all due respect, Mr. Beck, I was in California when the lights went out and I've had to kill more than ten men to get this far. I know how to use this gun. You need to let go of my arm, take a step back and shut your big mouth. If those guards come in here because of you, I won't hesitate to put a bullet in your brain before I kill them!"

Mr. Beck's mouth gaped open in shock but before he could respond, a new voice rang out in the dead silence that had filled the barn after Alex's warning.

"You have three seconds to take your hands off of my daughter before I tell her to go ahead and shoot."

Alex kept her eyes on her target but her heart swelled with joy at the sound of her father's voice. Mr. Beck must have seen something in Alex's eyes that convinced him because he dropped her arm and stepped back. She continued to stare coldly at the man until he dropped his gaze. Only then did she holster her gun and look around at all the other men staring back at her.

"I promise I will answer as many questions as I can after I speak with my father. I know you all want to know what's going on, but I haven't seen him since before this happened and...I really need a hug from my dad," she pleaded with them all.

Most faces softened and nodded, but she noticed that Mr. Beck looked furious and he had his eyes on the gun at her hip. Her hand automatically went to it and she challenged him with a hard look. There was another tense silence until two friends of her father's stepped forward and took Mr. Beck's arms. They were big men and Alex knew both of them worked with her dad on the volunteer fire fighting team. They nodded reassuringly at her and led her old gym teacher away. Only then did Alex turn and look at her dad. He was standing in the door of his office and he smiled when their eyes met. She took a step towards him and she could hear the love in his voice as he said her name before his eyes rolled back in his head and he crumpled to the ground.

Chapter Nine

Alex froze on the spot and a soft keening sound came from her throat. Dr. Mack was at her father's side in seconds and he waved over another man. Alex watched as they picked her dad up and carried him into the office and out of sight. Her mind and heart were paralyzed into inaction and she didn't know how long she stood there before Dr. Mack was shaking her arm.

"Alex, Alex, he's okay! He just fainted. He has a high fever and getting up just took the strength from him. Come in to the office."

Alex numbly followed the doctor into the office and saw her dad lying on a pallet made up of hay with an old horse blanket thrown over it. His face was pale white except for two flushed red spots on his cheeks from the fever. When his eyes fluttered open and focused on her, the paralysis that held her broke and she rushed forward to kneel beside him. Her voice was lost in the joy of just looking at him. His hand came up and pulled off her cap, dropping it to the floor, and then settled softly on her red curls. His eyes welled up with tears and he said her name on a breath before his strength left him again and his arm fell to his side.

Alex grabbed his hand and lifted it to her cheek. "Dad...daddy, I'm sorry I took so long."

A faint smile of amusement flickered across his face. "I knew you would make it home. I never doubted it once. My firecracker, did you run the whole way?"

She gasped out a sobbing laugh at the nickname he had given her as a child. "Not quite, but we did have to bike for a few days until we found transportation."

His eyebrows raised in question. "We? Who's with you?"

Alex settled down beside him. "The whole gang made it, dad, and a few others too." She frowned at as she remembered the situation. "We're going to save the town. We've been scouting all day and we'll put a plan together to free everyone."

Panic flared up in his eyes. "Alex, no. You kids need to get away from here. This gang is ruthless. You kids need to get somewhere safe."

Alex started to shake her head. "Dad...I...we aren't kids anymore. We...I've had to do things to get here that..." She hung her head in shame and couldn't go on.

He gripped her hand tighter. "I heard what you said to Beck. The men you killed, were they trying to hurt you?" When she only nodded, he continued, "Then I want you to put it aside. You did what you had to do to survive. All that matters now is that you're safe. I need you to stay that way."

Alex looked into his face and saw how tired and weak he looked so she changed the subject.

"I brought you medicine! I brought everything Dr. Mack will need to get you back on your feet." She let go of his hand and took her pack off. Dr. Mack moved forward to join them and his eyes lit up when she started to pull out the supplies that she had brought. Alex handed him the blister packs of pills and he read the labels. The doctor nodded his head and started to pop the pills out right away. He handed some of them to Alex's dad and she grabbed her water bottle so he could wash them down.

The doctor was looking through the bandages and suture kit and he smiled at her. "This is perfect, Alex! Now I can reopen that wound and drain it before stitching it up. With the antibiotics and the antiseptic, I don't see why he wouldn't heal up. You took a big risk coming in here, but I think you probably saved your dad's life."

Alex leaned over and kissed her dad's cheek before turning back to the doctor. "There's more. I brought a thermos of warm beef broth for dad and I also have some food for the rest of you. I know it's not much but it was all that I could carry."

She pulled a handful of power bars and sesame snaps from the bag and held them out to the doctor. When he saw what she was holding, he nodded.

"Anything extra will help right now, and these are full of protein."

Alex dumped the pack upside down until there was a mound in front of the doctor. His eyes lit up and then he frowned. "I need you to take all the packaging with you when you leave. If any of the guards find them they will know someone's been here. In fact, you will have to take everything back with you. Start popping the pills out of these blister packs. They're different colours so don't worry about mixing them up." He handed her the pills and went to the door to wave someone over. Two men came in and their eyes went straight to the pile of food on the floor. Dr. Mack scooped the bars up and put them on the desk before addressing the two men.

"We need to pass these out to the rest of the men but every wrapper needs to stay in this office so Alex can take them with her when she leaves. We can't take a chance of the guards finding out she was here, so one of you get the men to line up and then start unwrapping and handing them out." The two men moved quickly to do as he said and he turned back to Alex. "Okay, maybe you should help them to speed it up. I'm going to work on your dad's leg now so you can take the garbage with you," he told her, as he ripped open the bandages, scalpel and suture kit.

Alex looked at her dad's face and saw a grimace of pain pass over it before her gaze dropped to the dirty rag tied around his leg. She swallowed past her dry throat and felt sweat form on her body. After cutting into Quinn's body when he was shot, she knew what was coming and was thankful that she could let a real doctor handle it.

She got up and went to the desk and started to unwrap the bars. Alex couldn't help but flinch every time she heard her father moan or gasp in pain, but she kept her eyes on the desk. The man who was helping her kept stealing glances at her and finally asked her what was on his mind.

"How did you get all the way back here from California? There are a couple of people in here that had kids on that school trip. Is the power out everywhere? Did the government help you?"

Alex looked at the doorway where men were lined up and accepting the small amount of food with smiles. She hadn't even considered the families of the students that had chosen to stay in the city when she and her friends had left. Clearing her throat, she gave him a quick rundown on what had happened, leaving out the more painful details.

"I don't know what's happening on the east coast but everything between here and California is affected. We walked and then biked out of the city area until we found a vehicle that would work. We got lucky and had some help, but there wasn't any government anywhere. Some of my friends found a sailboat on the coast and sailed up as far as Washington and walked most of the way through B.C. They didn't see anything different than we did overland. Um…only ten of us students left and tried to make it home. The rest stayed in the city to wait for help. I'm sorry…I don't know what happened to them."

The man was quiet and seemed to be processing everything she said so she checked on her dad and saw his eyes squeezed shut in pain. The doctor was putting stitches in an ugly gash in his leg so she went to his side and took his hand and tried to distract him.

"Dad, Emily and David and some others took a different route than I did and they went through Merritt. They saw Peter and Susan and stayed with them for a night. They're both fine and they plan on heading here after Susan has the baby."

Her father smiled through gritted teeth and breathed out, "Thank God! Your mother will be so happy to hear that. She's been going out of her mind with worry not knowing what was happening with you kids."

"You've seen Mom? Is she okay?" Alex asked excitedly.

"Yes, we get to see our families once a week on Sundays. She's holding up but this has been hard on her. The not knowing what happened to her kids has been worse than the gang taking over the town. Your mother's a strong woman. She can handle anything as long as she knows her babies are safe."

As the doctor continued to work on his leg, they talked about the other families and what he knew about each. She watched his eyes slowly flutter as the painkillers started to take effect, so she leaned over and kissed him on his forehead.

"I love you, dad."

A faint smile crossed his face and then his breathing deepened and he was out. Alex took a minute to compose herself before turning to the doctor. He was finished stitching the wound and wrapping it with the clean bandages. He noticed she was watching him and saw that his patient had fallen asleep.

"You did good, Alex. This will make all the difference. He should heal up just fine now."

Alex was looking at the clean white bandage. "Will that give us away? Where will you tell the guards you got the bandages from?" she asked worriedly.

"Don't worry about that. I'm going to leave it for tonight, but in the morning I'll cover it with this rag. They'll never notice."

Alex glanced at the door and saw that the lineup was gone. There was a mound of wrappers on the desk so she stood up and began to stuff them back into her pack. Dr. Mack cleaned up the medical supplies and brought them over to her. Alex looked around the room for anything they might have missed and saw the thermos on the floor beside her sleeping father.

"Is there any way you can keep this? If he hasn't eaten because he hasn't been able to work, he will need something on his stomach with the medication he will be taking, right?"

Dr. Mack nodded his head and took the thermos from her. "Yes, he will need it. I should be able to hide it without too much trouble. I also kept a couple of the power bars for him. He will need the protein in them to help get his strength back." He looked at Alex with regret, "You have to get going, Alex. You've been here for almost an hour already. I don't want you to worry. I promise I will take care of your dad for you."

Alex reached out and took his hand. "We are going to get you all out of here, Dr. Mack! I don't know what the plan is yet, but I think it will be either Saturday night or Sunday. Just hold on of few more days. Okay?"

"Oh, Alex, please be careful! I know you kids want to help but trust me when I tell you your parents would rather be locked up and know you guys are safe and free. It's such a huge risk going up against these animals!"

Alex's eyes hardened and she looked him dead in the eyes. "Some risks are worth taking, no matter what the cost."

"Just be careful. I can't come and patch you up if one of you gets hurt." With a squeeze of her hand, Alex let the doctor pull her to her feet. She looked down on her sleeping father once more before following the doctor out of the office.

Back in the main part of the barn, almost all of the men were sitting or lying on any available floor space. When Alex walked out, all eyes turned to her. She was trying to find the words to reassure them when Dr. Mack addressed them.

"Listen up everyone! Alex needs to get going, she's already been here too long. She has told me everything that she knows right now and we can talk about it after we get her out of here. The most important thing is that everyone keeps their mouth shut about this little visit. Her group is trying to put a plan together to free us all and their biggest advantage right now is that they have surprise on their side." He paused and drilled a look at Mr. Beck who looked away in disgust before continuing. "I need a couple of tall guys to help Alex get back up that rope, so clear a space."

There was shuffling as the men moved away from the area where the rope hung down. Alex knew she didn't need any help to climb the rope but smiled gratefully at her father's two firefighting friends that came forward to give her a boost. As she walked through the men to the rope she was humbled by every man she passed as they reached out to touch or pat her. There were many, "Be safe's and thank you's", as she passed them. Taking one more look around she gave a sad smile and a little wave before stepping into one of the firefighters cupped hands and shimmying up the rope. When she got to the top and the pulley she swung a leg up and hooked it over the cross beam. Once again she was grateful for her gymnastic training. With her backpack empty and lighter she had an easier time balancing and was soon over the rail and back in the loft, after pulling the rope back up and rewrapping it around the beam. Pausing to look back, her eyes darted to the office door. She had done all she could for her father and she just prayed it was enough to get him through until they were free.

Going back out the hayloft door was more difficult than coming in even without having to fight with the latch. She had to back out on to the elevator and brace herself on her knees so she could pull the two boards out with her. Being as quiet as she could, she still winced at every creak of the metal but she trusted Josh to alert her if any of the guards had left the house. Once the door was closed again, she slipped each two by four back in their brackets. There was nothing she could do about relatching the door but given how lax the guards seemed to be, she didn't think they'd ever notice it. As she inched her way back down the elevator, she thought about how over confident the gang was by not patrolling or checking on their prisoners. A grim smile crossed her face as her feet hit the ground. They would use that confidence against the gang.

Hearing footsteps approaching, she ducked down beside the elevator and waited in the deep shadows to make sure it was Josh. When he walked past her hiding spot she gave a soft whistle to alert him and stepped out beside him. They dashed towards the trees and soon where back at the tree that hid the radios and

Alex's rifle. When everything was packed back up and shouldered, she turned to Josh.

"Thanks for coming and having my back," she told him with gratitude.

"Yeah, yeah but I get the shower first!"

"Shower? We have a shower?!" she asked in excitement.

Josh playfully punched her in the shoulder. "See what I gave up to come out here? You owe me big time...race you!"He took off crashing through the trees.

As Alex started to run, she let go of all her worries and for just a few minutes let herself be the girl she used to be, running after her friend through the trees.

Chapter Ten

Lisa woke to the sound of rain on the camper's roof. It was a soothing sound and she pulled the sleeping bag higher up around her ears to stay in the warmth of it for a few more minutes. She flashed back two nights before and the news they had all supplied from their scouting. Everyone had been relieved by the news that Alex had brought back about their mothers and siblings, everyone except Lisa and Cooper. He knew his father's fate but Lisa didn't know anything about what had happened to her parents. She was pretty sure her father had been in Calgary when the pulse hit, as he had his main office there, but her mother didn't travel in the same social circles as her new friends' parents so they didn't know her.

Lisa couldn't help but wonder if her mother had changed. Had the hardship of living without electricity and modern conveniences made her a better person like it had her daughter, or had she found someone to take care of her like she had her whole life? Lisa hoped her mother had changed, because right now she felt emptiness inside whenever she thought of her mother. It would really be nice if that could be filled by love and concern. She pushed aside what she knew deep down that she would never have, and thought about the plans for the day.

Yesterday, they had driven over an hour west into one of the many provincial parks in the area and found a secluded spot deep in the forest to do some target practice. Lisa had never fired a gun before and she had been nervous. Emily and David both had experience shooting rifles, so they had held the handguns with more confidence and it had only taken them a few practice shots before they were hitting the tree they were targeting. Quinn had been very patient with Lisa as he stood behind her and adjusted her grip and stance. He told her what to do and what to be prepared for but she still couldn't help herself from closing her eyes and flinching when she first pulled the trigger. After a dozen shots she was still too intimidated to come anywhere close to the tree trunk she was aiming for.

Quinn was showing her once again how to reload the gun when Josh started making jokes about her.

"Forget it, Quinn. Just give her some pom-poms and she can throw them at the bad guys! She's never going to hit that tree, probably afraid she'll break a nail or something!"

The old Lisa surfaced at his taunts and she wanted so badly to crush him like a bug with her trademark sarcastic venom, but she was trying to leave that girl behind in this new world so she ignored him. He kept at it and she felt her anger rise with every word.

"Hey, Lisa, maybe you can stand on one of the buildings roofs and distract the bad guys with a cheer. You could do a high kick and a cartwheel. That'll really show them!" Josh taunted with a laugh.

When Quinn handed her the loaded gun, her temper was barely suppressed and in one motion she brought the gun up and fired without pause until it clicked empty. She was so pissed at Josh that she didn't even acknowledge the fact that she had hit the tree dead-on with four shots. She glanced at Josh when he let out a rebel yell and was completely confused by his cheerful expression. Seconds ago the guy was throwing nasty insults her way and now he was doing a funky happy dance? What was with this guy?

Josh danced over to Lisa with a big grin and held up his hand for a high five. When she just stared at him blankly, he put on a fake pout.

"Aww, come on, Lisa, it worked, didn't it?"

"What? What worked?" she asked, completely lost.

"I got you mad, right? I got you out of your head so you would just shoot. You were over-thinking it! It worked too. You hit your target four times!" Josh grinned and turned her to point at the tree she had shot.

"I hit it? I hit it four times." She turned to Josh and beamed a huge smile. "I did! I hit it four times!" she said excitedly.

Emily walked over and put her hand on Lisa's shoulder before giving Josh a bemused look.

"I really do love you, Josh, but do you have to be a total idiot?" she asked.

He gave her a wounded look. "Hey, I was trying to help!"

Emily just shook her head. "Yup, you pissed off a girl with a loaded gun. Smart, really smart." She turned to Lisa. "If you have to shoot him, aim for his feet. We still need him for a few things!"

The two girls broke out in laughter as Josh stalked away pretending to be offended and Lisa felt the last of her nerves flow away. She looked at Quinn and winked.

"How about we try a bigger gun?"

When he threw his hands up in mock surrender, she laughed again and followed Emily over to the rifles.

The rest of the shooting practice went well and they all got comfortable firing the more powerful assault rifles on all three settings. They wouldn't win any awards in accuracy but at least they all now knew how to use them. By the time they made it back to their base, it was late afternoon and the weather had turned to rain, so they stayed in camp and discussed different ideas of their plan. They all agreed that they needed to do more scouting and get more information but after seeing and hearing about how their families were being treated they wanted to make their move fairly soon.

Lisa felt the camper shift as one of the girls got up and she pulled her sleeping bag down enough so that her eyes could peak over the edge. Alex was up and moving around the small kitchen area. Lisa was still surprised at how much she admired the girl after having such contempt for her when they went to school together. It was amazing how one month had changed her perspectives in life, and what she had looked down on before became things she admired.

The pressure of her bladder told her it was time to get up so she unzipped her bag and shuddered at the cold air that flew in. Spring mornings in Alberta were far from warm, so she was quick to layer up before shuffling in her thick socks to the tiny bathroom in the camper. They had no power or water working in the camper but the toilet emptied directly in to a holding tank so they had agreed to use it at night and first thing in the morning. Quinn had scavenged blue portable waste containers from some of the RVs they had looted and had explained to her how you could empty the holding tanks into them and then wheel them away to dump. She was still marvelling at all the things they had to do now, with no power, just to meet their basic needs. She used a bucket of water that was in the bathtub to rinse the toilet, and a bottle of water by the sink to brush her teeth and clean her hands and face before joining Alex at the small dining table.

Alex had brought her sleeping bag with her from her bunk and was zipped into it on the bench. She gave Lisa a warm smile and pulled it up higher when a draft of cold air sneaked in to it.

"I never thought I would be this grateful for a camper in the woods! Can you imagine sleeping in a tent right now? We would be popsicles! You and

Quinn have my many thanks for hauling this sucker back here."

Lisa shivered, "At least it's not snowing. Remember last year? We had a huge party planned at the lake for May long weekend and we ended up getting something like ten centimeters."

Alex shuddered, "Bite your tongue! I don't even want to think about snow. I'm already having nightmares about how we're going to survive next winter without central heat!"

"Mmmmm, central heat," Emily muttered as she shuffled in to the room and squeezed in beside Lisa on the dining table bench. She opened the blanket she had wrapped around herself and spread part of it over Lisa so they could huddle under it together. With a huge yawn, she asked "What's the plan for today?"

Dara answered her. She had followed Emily into the room and was looking out the small window above the sink.

"Looks like the plan is to get very wet and very cold." She turned and joined the other three girls at the table with a look of disgust at the weather outside. Alex moved over to give her space and they huddled together for a minute as they slowly woke up.

They started to hear sounds from outside so Alex parted the blinds and checked to see who was moving around out there. With a smirk at Dara, she told them what she had seen.

"Looks like your boyfriend is on breakfast duty, he's set up the camp stove under their awning."

Dara let out a sigh. "Well, in that case, we should…stay right here and let him do it!"

Alex laughed, "You know he can burn water, right?"

Dara gave a one shouldered shrug. "That's okay, he has other talents."

Alex gaped at her. "Seriously? He finally made a move?"

Dara gave a smug smile. "He might be a goof, but man oh man, can that boy kiss!"

Alex held up a hand in a stop gesture. "Okay, okay, I'm happy for you guys but please no details! Josh is way too much like a brother to me for that. Can I just say…EEEWWW!"

Dara laughed, "Fair enough. What about you? Have Quinn or Cooper made any moves again?"

Alex rolled her eyes. "No, thank God. I think they put all that on hold while we sort out what to do about our families, and now that I think about it, Cooper has barely even spoken to me in days."

Dara frowned and looked down at the table before glancing at the other girls. "Yeah, he's really struggling right now. He blames himself for what his dad did to the town and then…something happened when we were scouting." She took a deep breath and explained how the two girls they had first approached had reacted. "He took it really hard."

Lisa was surprisingly the first to respond. "That's total bull! It's not his fault at all!"

Alex shook her head. "No, it's not. We will have to find a way to make him understand and we'll all have his back if anyone says different. Agreed?" When all the girls nodded, Alex peaked out the blinds again. "Oh, crap! We've got to get out there!"

At the other girls' concerned faces, Alex told them with a grim expression, "Josh just put a frying pan on the stove!"

They all scrambled to get out from behind the table and get dressed. They knew they were in for charred pancake pucks if they didn't get Josh away from that stove.

The girls saved breakfast from disaster and everyone ate as many pancakes as possible. They knew they would be burning up calories in the cold, wet weather as they scouted out the roadblocks set up around town. The plan was to stick together today and use the truck and bikes to circle the town. They would drive out a good distance and then use their bikes to get in closer to town on the main roads. It would take too long to walk around the town at a safe distance and check each road for guards, so Quinn would drive and drop teams of two at each road starting on the north side of town before circling back to pick up the first team and moving on to the east and then south side before finishing the loop on the west side and returning to base. Now that they had the radios, it would be easier to communicate if any of the teams ran in to trouble.

They decided that Quinn and Lisa would travel in the truck because his leg was still healing and she was the least experienced with a firearm. They loaded up six bikes in the back of the truck and it made for a tight fit with three in the cab and five in the back, but it was better than walking.

There wasn't a lot of talking for the five in the back, with the wind and rain blowing down on them. They kept their hoods up and heads down until they felt the truck slowing down. The first road they were going to scout ran in a north south direction. The road ran between Emily and Josh's properties so they would team up to bike down it. The plan was for them to bike as close to town as they thought was safe and then use the fields on either side of the road to get close enough to see if there was a roadblock set up. Everyone in the group knew the most likely roads that would be watched but they had to make sure they didn't miss a group of guards. They needed to account for as many as possible if any plan they came up with was to be successful.

Josh helped Emily down from the truck bed and David and Cooper helped to pass down their bikes. Once they were ready, Josh reached under his jacket and turned on the walkie talkies so Quinn could contact them if anything went wrong. With a quick wave, the two pedalled away and Quinn drove to the next road that led into town and dropped off David and Alex. As soon as they were away, he drove to the area they had first scouted on the main highway when they had sent Cooper to the roadblock. There had been four guards there when Cooper had biked up and talked to his father's friend but they wanted to confirm the number was the same.

Cooper and Dara were going to scout this location and Dara gave a shiver as rain slid down her back when she stepped out of the warm interior of the truck. They unloaded their bikes and headed down the road to the trees that they had used the first time to spy on the roadblock.

Quinn and Lisa did a U-turn in the truck and headed back to where they had first dropped off Josh and Emily. When they made it back Quinn pulled to the side of the road and shut the engine off. He was feeling guilty for sitting in the warm, dry truck while his friends were out in the cold rain putting themselves in danger. As if she had read his mind, Lisa brought up the next part of the plan.

"I'm not looking forward to being out in that rain, but it will feel good to be contributing. I kind of feel like we're getting spoiled in this truck."

Quinn smiled at her. "I was just feeling guilty about that, but you're right. We'll be just as wet and miserable once we get to the south side."

Using the bikes only worked on this side of town where it was mainly farm fields and country roads. The south side of town backed on to forest land with a golf course in between and only one main road running through it to enter the town. They had decided to scout out the golf course to see if the gang was using it for gardens like they had with the park. They needed to know if they were holding people in that area. They would leave the truck in the forest on one of the oil well lease roads and walk in on foot through the trees. The entire group planned on scouting it out and they would split up and circle the golf course before checking the main highway's roadblock for numbers.

Lisa broke into Quinn's thoughts, "There they are!"

Josh and Emily rode towards them and dismounted from their bikes. Quinn flipped up his jacket's hood and stepped out to give them a hand loading the bikes back into the truck. Once they were secured, Quinn suggested that Josh and Emily get into the cab to warm up. Josh could drive them to the next pick up spot and get warmed up.

Josh shook his head. "Thanks, man, but we're soaked through. We would just get the seats wet. Besides, you need to keep that leg warmed up for when we hit the south side. After that, we'll all be wet, and I'll take you up on that offer on the way home."

Emily agreed by hopping into the bed of the truck and making a "let's go" motion with her hand. Quinn frowned in guilt, but agreed and got back into the truck and started it up. He knew how bad his leg would be aching after they scouted out the golf course on foot. The damp weather was already aggravating his leg injury and he was in for much worse.

David and Alex were already waiting by the side of the road when they came to pick them up. Josh waved Quinn back into the truck and he and David loaded up the next pair of bikes. With a bang on the side of the truck to let him know they were ready, Quinn drove them to the last pick up spot. The four in the back huddled together for warmth as they waited on the side of the road for Cooper and Dara to make an appearance. It didn't take long before they were spotted heading back towards the truck and their bikes were quickly loaded up. Quinn did another U-turn and headed away from the roadblock area. They would have to do a large circle around it to keep the sound of the truck's engine from being heard.

Once they had gone around far enough, Quinn turned on to a road that would take them back west towards the town. They had been driving for ten minutes and were getting closer to the area they were going to hide the truck in when a sign came into view that had him slowing the truck. He pulled over to the side of the road and hopped out to talk to his friends in the back. Dara and Lisa jumped out of the cab and joined him.

"Hey guys, I know we were going to park back in the trees and walk in to the golf course but I just remembered that the dump's northwest end backs almost against the eighteenth hole. What if we park in the dump and walk from there? It would put us a lot closer."

Josh lifted his hood up so he could meet Quinn's eyes. "I'm up for anything that will mean less walking in this miserable weather. There's a bunch of junked cars in there that David and I pull parts from. We can put the truck back between some of them and it should go unnoticed. I doubt these guys are using the dump anyway, so let's do it."

Everyone else agreed so Quinn jumped back in behind the steering wheel and took off. He made the turn on to the access road to the dump and followed it to the gates and past the small office shack. He didn't give much thought to the gates being opened and drove deeper in on the dirt pathways that led to different dumping areas. When he saw the junk cars and trucks he drove slowly past until he found an opening between an abandoned school bus and a rust covered cargo van.

They all jumped out of the truck and walked back on the pathway they had driven on. Josh led the way and they followed him through the area towards the northwest corner. Every now and then a gust of wind would hit them that brought the faint smell of rot and the girls would wrinkle their noses. They came to the perimeter fence and Josh pulled a pair of wire cutters from his pack. They knew they might have to deal with fences on this trip so they had come prepared. It was easier to cut through the fences than to try and have everyone climb over them and risk being seen. The perimeter of the dump was separated from the golf course by fifty feet of trees and they all were happy with the coverage.

When they came to the tree line, it was clear that at least this end of the course hadn't been cultivated for growing. The once manicured lawns were starting to go wild, but they still looked like a golf course. The group split up with each team going separate ways to scout the whole course. Lisa, Emily, David and Cooper headed north towards town and would use the trees that had been planted between the backyards of houses backing on to the course for cover as they moved west. The others would travel south and circle west to check out the clubhouse and further on, the road that ran beside the course into town for a roadblock.

Lisa's group stayed in the trees until they merged with the strip that protected the homes backing on to the course from any wild golf balls. They headed west and tried to stay in the middle of the narrow strip of trees in case there was anyone in the houses that might look out and see them. They had been traveling for a while without seeing anything, when Cooper came to a stop and raised his hand so the others would stop also. He looked back at them and then pointed ahead towards the backyard of a house further on. There was a trail of smoke from some sort of fire coming from one of the homes. Lisa squinted through the rain and let out a small gasp. When all eyes swung her way she swallowed hard.

"That's my house! That smoke is coming from my backyard!" she exclaimed.

Cooper frowned and looked back at the smoke trail. "Is there a fire pit in your backyard?"

Lisa nodded. "Yes, my dad put it in a few years ago for company parties. My mother hated it and had it replaced with a decorative propane model though. She hated the smell of woodsmoke getting in her hair and clothes."

"Well, it's a wood burning fire now. What kind of fence runs along the back?" Cooper asked.

Lisa though about it for a minute before replying. "It's a chainlink fence with plastic wooden strips woven through it. It's only about five feet tall though and it has a wrought iron gate in it."

Cooper looked at the others. "Okay, let's get closer but move to the golf course side of the trees. There doesn't seem to be anyone on the course so we should be good from that direction. We'll take a look and see if anyone's in the yard from there."

The closer they got to Lisa's yard, the tighter her stomach got with nerves. She had no idea why the gang would be using her family's home when so many others sat empty. When they were directly behind her yard's fence, they crouched down and waited for any sounds to be made from the yard. When nothing happened for a few minutes, Lisa moved a few feet forward and over to look through the gate. From her angle she could see that the backyard was empty, but there was a fire going in the pit with a large pot suspended over it. She couldn't smell any food being cooked in the air but there was steam rising from the pot. Movement caught her attention as the back door opened and slammed shut. A teenage girl crossed the deck and down the stairs. She walked straight to the fire and picked up a long wooden spoon and dipped it in. When the girl flipped her long bangs away from her face, Lisa's eyes grew large. She flinched when Cooper put his hand on her shoulder from behind.

"Do you know who that is?" he asked, almost directly in her ear.

Lisa nodded. "It's Payton Abrahams. She… was my assistant Captain on the cheerleading team. I have no idea why she's at my house though."

They stayed crouched down and watched the girl stir whatever was in the pot. Lisa studied her former teammate's face. They were not what you would call friends, as Lisa never really had any close friends, but the two girls had spent a long time together on the cheerleading team. Payton absently stirred the pot while looking blankly into the distance. The slump of her shoulders was a far cry from the confident cheerleader who used to walk the halls of the high school. When the girl reached a hand up and wiped away tears, Lisa moved forward. Cooper tightened his hand on her shoulder to stop her but she shrugged it off and moved closer to the fence.

All that separated Lisa from her back fence was a strip of overgrown lawn and a paved walk way. Lisa scanned the back windows of her house and saw that every one was covered by closed blinds. She looked back at Payton and saw her chest hitch in a silent sob. Without even looking back at the others, she stepped out of the trees and dashed across the pathway, and crouched down behind her fence. She duck-walked forward until she was at the edge of the gate and she could peek around it. Checking the windows one more time for movement and finding none, Lisa made a "Psst!" noise.

The girl in the yard reacted like she had been hit and flinched violently before looking at the house and frantically searching the yard for the source of the noise. She spotted Lisa's head peeking around the gate and did a double-take with her mouth gaping open.

"Payton…it's me, Lisa. What are you doing here?" Lisa called softly.

The girl looked desperately back at the house before hissing in the direction of the gate. "I don't know how you got back here, Lisa, but you need to get away! Your mother…"

The sound of the back door opening cut her off and she frantically started to stir at the pot in front of her, keeping her eyes down and away from the gate.

Lisa yanked her head back from the gate. Her heart was pounding and her eyes flashed to the trees but she couldn't see any of her friends. The voice calling across the yard cut straight through her.

"What is taking so long out here, Payton? I know you are upset but you still have many more chores to do before our guests get here tonight!"

Lisa had no control over her legs as they straightened her into a standing position. She stepped in front of the gate and faced her mother. She was mildly surprised by her mother's appearance. The woman looked exactly the same as when she had driven Lisa to the airport a month ago. Flawless makeup, and not a hair out of place complemented the designer dress and high heeled shoes. It was like her mother hadn't been living without electricity for the last month.

Lisa's mother was alerted by her movements and her head turned to meet her daughter's gaze. They stood facing each other like that for what felt to Lisa like hours before her mother's expression altered slightly with raised eyebrows and she walked closer to the gate.

"Lisa...this is unexpected." After a brief pause she continued. "I wouldn't personally have chosen such a style for your hair, but thankfully you have the eyes and cheekbones to carry it."

Lisa's mouth dropped open in shock as her mother studied her before she sputtered out, "That's it? That's all you have to say to me after all this time? Mother, what is going on?"

The woman frowned, "Please, Lisa. You know how I feel about dramatics. Of course I'm relieved to see you made it home safely. If you wish to discuss your trip then come in to the house. It will take some work to get you cleaned up and ready for later."

"What are you talking about?! Why aren't you at the school with the others? Who're these guests you're talking about?" Lisa asked in confusion.

Payton made a horrified sound, bringing the woman's focus back to her. "Payton! Go inside and get to work. Oh, and Payton? Not a word to anyone about this," Lisa's mother ordered.

Payton dropped the spoon and raced for the backdoor. When she reached it, she turned back and behind the woman's back, violently shook her head at Lisa in warning before slipping back into the house and closing the door.

Lisa refocused on her mother with a look of confusion. Before she could ask another question, her mother started to explain.

"As you know, I'm not accustomed to manual labour, so I made an arrangement with the men who are now in charge of our town. I get to live here in our home with a few other women and enjoy some extra privileges and luxuries in exchange for certain services. You would do well here with me. Come into the house and we can start getting you ready."

Lisa stared at her mother. She wasn't even surprised, but just to be clear she asked, "You started a whorehouse and you want me to be one of your whores?"

Her mother frowned and waved her hand dismissively. "Really, Lisa, don't be ugly about it! I did what I had to do to survive. Now make your decision. Either come in to the house or leave the area and find someone else to take you in." She looked back at the house and checked her watch. "Hurry up! I'm expecting some men to come and remove...some garbage. If you aren't interested, I suggest you leave the area before you don't have a choice."

Lisa's head was shaking back and forth as she stepped back from the gate. She tried to think of the words she wanted to say but found that the emptiness inside of her heart had taken over her whole body so all that came out was, "Goodbye, mother," in a flat tone.

Her mother had no expression on her face as she watched Lisa back away. Just as she was about to turn around and leave her mother stopped her.

"Lisa! Your father was in Calgary that day. He never came home so I don't know what happened to him. You could try to look for him if you aren't staying here."

When Lisa only nodded, her mother turned and walked back into the house without a look back. Lisa stared at the closed door of her home and felt nothing. She vaguely wondered if she was as cold as her mother to not feel anything about what just happened. She shoved the thought aside when she heard Emily quietly calling her name and turned and slipped back into the trees to join her friends. The only people she had left in this hard new world.

Emily's face was filled with concern and compassion and she pulled Lisa in to a hug before pulling back and studying her face. "I'm so sorry, Lisa. Are you okay?"

Lisa pulled away and nodded before turning to the others. "I'm fine and I'm sorry for going over there. I know it put us all at risk. I promise it won't happen again. We should get moving if we want to meet back with the others." She quickly changed the subject and then started to walk in the direction they were headed. She couldn't bear the looks of pity she saw in her friends' eyes.

Chapter Eleven

Alex and her group circled their side of the golf course on the way to the clubhouse. They had more tree coverage than the other group so they made good time and were able to walk more confidently through the trees without risk of being seen. They saw no sign of the grounds being used for farming or gardening, and Josh put out the theory that they didn't have enough man power to guard any more areas than what they had already seen being used. Alex was happy and hopeful that they wouldn't be running into any guards. Quinn was moving well and had no problem keeping up with them, but she knew if it came to them having to run, he would be struggling with his still healing leg. She glimpsed a reflection of light through the trees and slowed down.

They approached the tree line cautiously and stopped just before reaching it. There was a large parking lot separating them from the clubhouse that had a few abandoned, dead cars. Nothing moved or made any sound in the ten minutes they spent watching it. After deciding that they were alone, Josh dashed across the lot until he was up against the building. He made his way to the corner and peered around it before looking back to the trees and waving them forward. On the other side of the building was a staging area where golfers would pick up their golf cart and start the course. It was empty as well. The pulse had happened way before golf season would have started so the only people around at the time it had happened would have been administrative and maintenance people.

The group crossed the lawn and reentered the trees. They followed the tree line as it wound around the course until it turned back towards the north and town. They continued west through the trees until they saw the pavement of the road ahead. This was the only road coming from the south that ran into the town. If there was a roadblock, it would be somewhere on it.

Alex took the binoculars from her pack, looped the strap over her head and tucked them into her jacket before crawling out of the trees and through the ditch to the edge of the pavement. The cold wet grass soaked through her pants, but she ignored it and used the binoculars to scan the road. She could make out the first buildings at the beginning of town and the road was clear in that direction. Looking south, all she could see was trees as the road curved out of sight. Deciding that she didn't need to crawl and get even wetter, she stood up and walked back to the trees to join the others. After she told them what she had seen, they all turned and headed south through the trees. There was one road to cross that ran in front of the golf course clubhouse. Crossing it was a quick dash and then they moved further away from the road as they approached the curve in case the roadblock was right around the bend.

The sound of a car door slamming validated their caution. Moving low and slow, the group moved further around the bend in the trees until the next stretch of road was revealed. An older model pickup truck and a rusty sedan were across the road facing each other. Alex pulled the glasses from her shirt and zeroed in on the pickup where a man in a rain slicker was standing talking to two men in the cab of the truck. She swung the glasses to the car but the rain on the windows obscured her view. She passed the glasses to Josh.

"Two in the truck, one on the road but I can't get a good look in to the car with the rain."

He nodded and brought the glasses up to his eyes. Everyone waited in silence in the rain. Josh and Emily had seen a roadblock with four men on the road they had scouted on the north side but Alex and David had rode their bikes almost to the first buildings in town without seeing anyone. There had been four men blocking the main highway on both ends of town and Alex was willing to bet that they would discover only one more man in the sedan.

The wet weather was starting to really chill them now that they weren't moving and a faint rustle had Alex turning to see Quinn slowly stretching his damaged leg. She sent him a reassuring smile and turned back to the road just as the man chatting with those in the truck turned and walked back to the car. He opened the door and was going to get in when someone from the truck yelled something to him from the open window. The man standing in the open door took two steps back towards the truck to reply and it left a clear view into the interior of the sedan. Alex saw Josh lean forward with the glasses until the guard got in and shut the door. He lowered the binoculars from his face and turned to the others using a waving motion to get them moving back the way they had come.

They backtracked through the trees and once they had made a good distance back towards the golf course, Josh told them what he had seen.

"There was a guy in the passenger seat and I had a partial view of the backseat and it seemed empty. There might have been someone else in there but I doubt it. So far we have seen teams of four at all the roadblocks and if they were going to post more than that, it would be on the main highway, not this secondary road."

Quinn nodded. "I agree. Let's get back and meet up with the others. We'll have a better idea of what to do next once we get the information written on the map."

Dara's teeth started to chatter at that moment and Alex shivered in sympathy.

"Come on, at least when we're moving we warm up a bit." Alex said, and they trudged back to the golf course.

They saw no one as they back tracked along the course and skirted the clubhouse. Alex imagined being wrapped up under a mound of blankets holding a hot cup of coffee. She couldn't wait to be back at the camper and out of this miserable weather. Her heart had a pang of guilt that she would be worried about her discomfort, when she remembered that her fellow townspeople wouldn't have that option if they were being forced to work outside.

She almost walked into Josh's back when he stopped in front of her. Her head came up and she moved out from behind him to see what was ahead. Alex smiled at the other group when she saw them waiting by the cut in the fence that led back to the dump. They looked just as wet and miserable as she felt, but something else seemed off about the group. Emily and David looked sad and Cooper looked like he could smash something, judging by his clenched fists and the expression on his face. Lisa's face was completely blank and her eyes were a million miles away.

Alex stepped forward and asked, "What? What happened?"

Cooper opened his mouth to speak but then shut it with a snarl and turned away. It was Lisa who filled them in with what they had discovered at her old house, and her tone was flat and without emotion as she recounted what her mother had said.

Alex stood staring at the girl. She couldn't even contemplate having a mother that was so unfeeling and cold. She struggled to find the right words to ease Lisa's pain but came up blank. Thankfully, Dara seemed to know exactly the right tone to use.

"That BITCH!" she spat with venom. "Maybe your mom and my mom and Cooper's dad should have had their own little club. The deadbeat parents club!"

Lisa's eyes widened at Dara's words and she tilted her head to the side in awe. Lisa had never had anyone be incensed on her behalf. She watched Dara stomp around and curse their parents before she turned and grabbed Lisa by the shoulders. Dara's eyes were filled with understanding and compassion.

"You listen to me, Lisa. That woman is nothing...nothing! WE are your family now and WE will always be your family!"

Something clicked inside of Lisa and she felt the words Dara spoke to be true and heartfelt. Lisa slowly started to nod and looked at the others staring back at her. A trembling smile crossed her lips as she met each of their eyes. She sucked in a ragged breath before speaking to them.

"This world sucks but I have more now than I did before. I have a family now. Before, all I had was a house with two strangers that I lived with. Thank you." Her face crumpled and the tears that had been locked inside were finally freed.

Alex and Emily moved forward and joined Dara, who had wrapped her arms around the sobbing girl. One by one the boys came forward and rubbed Lisa's back or squeezed her shoulder in comfort. Quinn took a step back. He had a small smile on his face. He knew all about making a new family, what you needed most was love.

Once the tears had been dried, they made their way through the cut fence and back in to the dump. They were all thinking about getting back to base and warming up when sounds of an engine starting up close by reached their ears. They scattered by instinct, and Alex dove behind an old rust covered refrigerator that had its door removed. She looked around frantically for the location of the vehicle but could only see a few of her friends taking cover. Alex tried to pinpoint where the sound was coming from, but her heart was pounding so hard in her ears it was all she could hear. Movement caught her eye and she looked over to see Josh waving everyone down. Her breath caught at how close he was to the main pathway that led out of the dump. Wherever the vehicle was, it would have to drive right past him to get to the gates. She crouched lower and kept her eyes on Josh. He was looking down the pathway away from her and she held her breath in fear when he flinched back and grabbed an old sheet of tin roofing and yanked it over him. Her eyes were wide open and she was afraid to blink as the sound of the motor got closer. She could see Josh's hiding place but not the dirt path that the vehicle was slowly driving on from her angle behind the fridge. Cold rain splashed in her face and eyes, making her duck her head down. The sound of the engine was loud, like it was right on top of them but then it gradually moved away. Everyone stayed where they were hiding for a good five minutes before Alex heard Josh call out the all clear.

They all met up at the crossways and as one looked towards the gates. The road was clear as far as they could see and they relaxed. Emily rubbed her face and looked at the others.

"That was close. I think I peed my pants a little bit!"

Josh let out a bark of laughter. "Yeah? Well that'll be easier to get out than the stain I just left in my underwear!"

A chorus of groans of disgust and laughter made Josh grin his trademark smile before he looked in the opposite direction, back where the vehicle had come from. He rubbed at his head in thought before turning back to the group.

"What were those guys doing here? If they were just tossing trash, why did they drive so far back? They could have just dumped it on the closest pile."

Lisa's head came up and she looked at her friends who had been with her at her parent's house.

"My mother! She said she was expecting men to come and remove some garbage. That's probably who it was."

Quinn nodded. "Okay, but Josh is right. Why didn't they just dump it on the first pile? Why go so far back?"

Josh waved his arm over his head in a forward motion and started walking. Over his shoulder he called back to them, "Only one way to find out!"

They were all tired, cold and wet and wanted to get back to base, but they needed all the information they could get on the gang, so if looking at their garbage would help, then that's what they would do. The dirt pathways that ran between mounds of junk had turned into a muddy mess but it also served them by clearly showing the tire tracks. With Josh in the lead they trudged after him. A cold gust of wind blew rain and a sickly stench in their faces. Alex wrinkled her nose at the smell and was surprised when Josh came to a dead stop about ten feet ahead of them. He whirled around and threw his hands up in a stop motion. His face had drained of all color and his eyes were horrified.

"Go back! I know what they were dumping and you guys don't want to see it!"

Alex looked at him in confusion. "What? Josh, what is it?"

He swallowed hard and sent her a pleading look. "Can't you smell it?"

Alex made a face and looked at her other friend's confused faces. "What? It's just rotting gar..." Her mind made the connection with the smell just as she was going to say garbage and her face turned to horror. "OH MY GOD!" She took off in a run straight at him. Josh threw his arm out to stop her but she dodged it and kept going until she came to a huge pit that had been dug in one of the garbage mounds. What she saw had her spinning away and bolting to the other side of the pathway to heave out the contents of her stomach. She heard feet pounding up to her and then sounds of some of the others puking as well.

Quinn let out a strangled yell of anguish and Cooper violently screamed, "SON OF A BITCH!"

Alex was bent over with her hands wrapped around her stomach when she heard Emily sobbing. She spit to clear her mouth and stood up and went to her friend, wrapping her in her arms. Dara was standing beside her, as pale as the death in the pit and silent hitches made her chest jerk so Alex grabbed her and pulled her close too.

The girls huddled together and felt their insides break into sad little pieces. Alex wished she had listened to Josh. She had only taken a quick glance down in to the pit of bodies but it was enough to sear the image in her brain forever.

Lisa was standing at the edge of the pit. She had her arms wrapped around herself and she was rocking back and forth mumbling over and over, "She said it was garbage. She said it was garbage."

Alex swallowed hard and pushed Emily into Dara's arms before going to Lisa and trying to pull her away. When she took the girls arm her head turned and the largest, emptiest eyes met hers. "Anne Marie is not garbage," she said flatly.

"Who's Anne Marie, Lisa?" Alex asked gently.

Lisa turned back to the pit and raised her hand to point. Alex didn't want to look but she couldn't help herself. Following Lisa's pointing finger she saw a body wrapped in a clean white sheet. It stood out like a beacon against the gray bodies it had been dumped on. The sheet was so clean and it was only just starting to dampen in the rain. The main part of the body was still wrapped in the sheet, but the head and one pale naked arm and shoulder had been exposed when it was tossed into the pit. Alex found her eyes moving over the swollen, bruised face. It had been beaten so badly that it was impossible to recognize who it was. The damaged face was surrounded by a halo of shiny, clean blond cork screw curls and a few curls that were matted with blood. Alex pulled her gaze away from the body and focused on Lisa.

"Are you sure you know her? Her face is hard to recognize. It could be anyone, Lisa."

Lisa shook her head. "See? On her shoulder? She has a four leaf clover tattoo. She was captain last year and she got it for luck before we went to Regionals. We won." Lisa trailed off.

David had joined them at the side of the pit and he was studying the bodies. His voice was strangled when he asked, "Alex, do you recognize those armbands?"

Alex looked where he was pointing. She wanted to run away and scrub her mind of what she was seeing, but the shock had worn off and she felt frozen with numbness as she looked at the grey arms and legs mixed together. She spotted what David was pointing at and as soon as she saw it she knew what it was and other arms with bands came into view. Her voice had no emotion in it. She felt dead inside when she answered him.

"They're from the nursing home. The bands have the patient's information and medications on them."

David didn't look up from the bodies. "My grandma is in there. She had dementia. She wouldn't have known what was happening. Did they just die or did they kill them?" he asked in a little boy voice.

Quinn and Josh pulled the three of them away from the pit and steered them down the pathway before Alex could answer him. It was for the best. She didn't think she could bear to tell him that they all had holes in their heads.

Chapter Twelve

Alex peeled her sodden clothing off her body and dropped it to the floor of the camper with a splat. Her skin was cold, clammy, and pale and she couldn't stop the tremors that coursed through her. She wrapped her naked body in a towel and attacked her dripping hair. Once it was no longer dripping she wrapped a dry towel around it and secured it like a turban. Everything she did since leaving the dump had been on autopilot. Her brain and body were numb from emotional overload. Climbing into her bunk, she piled blankets on top of herself and created a nest where she could hide for a while.

The ride back to base had been silent as they all dealt with what they had discovered. Alex had sat in the back of the truck with her back against the cab and her knees drawn up to her chest, staring at the countryside as it passed by. Everything looked grey and dismal to her, like all the color had been washed from the world. She kept seeing a repetitive motion out of the corner of her eye and when she finally turned her heavy head to look she saw Josh was clenching his hands into fists and opening them. He kept repeating the motion, making his knuckles flare white against the bone before releasing them. Her gaze slowly traveled up his arms in a detached way until they landed on his face. Here was color. His face was bone white except for two bright red flags across his cheek bones. Alex hardly recognized her friend. She had never seen such rage and anguish in his eyes before. He looked nothing like the goofy boy she had loved like a brother most of her life. If Alex had been capable of feeling anything right then, she might have been afraid for him. He looked like he was about to tear something apart with his bare hands. Dara leaned against him and raised her hands to cover his. His hand clenching stopped but he continued to stare at his hands so Alex let her gaze slide away back to the passing landscape.

Quinn drove them back to base without stopping to check on the last roadblock. He knew there was a good chance that one or more of his group wouldn't be able to restrain themselves from attacking the guards if they saw them now. They all needed some time to come to terms with what they had seen. As sad and angry as he was, he knew they needed cooler heads before they made any move against the men holding the town. When they pulled into base behind the camper van, everyone had scattered. Dara led Josh away into the trees, Emily and David went to the picnic table and sat in the rain just holding on to each other, Cooper paced around the campsite in angry strides before grabbing the axe and taking out his emotions by chopping up wood, and Lisa followed Alex into the girl's camper. Quinn absently rubbed at his aching thigh before turning and going into the camper van. Time…they just needed some time.

When Alex woke up, her eyes were swollen and aching, telling her she had been crying in her sleep. The cold numbness had left her body, she was warm under the blankets and there was a comforting weight pressed up against her back. She didn't know how long she had slept, but the camper was dark and she knew night had fallen. She shifted slightly, and the person against her stirred. With a sleepy voice, Emily asked, "What time is it?"

Alex drew her arm out of the warm cocoon to check her watch but it was too dark to see so she just shrugged against Emily and stayed silent. Emily's hand found Alex's under the blankets and they just laid beside each other lost in their own thoughts. Sounds drifted through the thin metal walls of the camper.

Alex could hear low murmurings and the snap of wood burning in the campfire. She thought they should get up and eat something but that meant facing the others and talking about what had happened earlier in the day and she wasn't ready for that. Emily didn't give her a choice when she shivered and snuggled closer to her friend.

"Do you think we will ever go back to the way we were before? You know, like normal kids who help out around the farm and have fun playing in the woods? Sometimes, I don't think I will ever feel like a kid again."

Alex unwillingly flashed back through all the things she had seen and done since leaving Disneyland.

"No. We will never be the same again. Nothing will ever be like it was before." she whispered, and felt Emily nod against her shoulder.

"Alex? Those people…at the dump. They were executed. Why? Why would the gang do that?"

Alex sighed sadly, "They were elderly and some of them were sick so the gang wouldn't have seen them as anything but extra mouths to feed."

Emily squeezed her hand. "I'm sorry, Alex. I know you knew a lot of them from volunteering there."

Alex thought about all the patients she had sat and read to or played cards with. She felt like she should cry for them but her heart had drained of tears and was filling back up with anger.

"It's such a waste! Do you know how much knowledge they threw away by killing those people? Those were the people that helped build our country. They knew how to work and fight and survive without modern conveniences. They lived this life we're in right now and flourished! Just because they got old doesn't mean they had no value!"

Emily sat up and swung her feet over the side of the bunk. "Come on, let's get dressed and get out there. We need to plan on how we're going to make them pay for what they did."

Alex felt goose bumps cover her body when Emily threw back the blankets to get up. She scrambled out and searched around for dry clothes to put on. She stumbled over her cold wet clothes that she had left in a heap on the floor. After she had dressed and thrown her messy hair into a ponytail, she picked them up and hung them to dry. Alex could tell that the rain had stopped since she could no longer hear it against the camper's metal roof, but the air was damp so she pulled on an extra jacket and stepped out into the campsite.

Everyone was sitting around the campfire eating, except Emily, who was over at the camp stove dishing up two bowls of pasta from the pot. She met Alex halfway and handed her the steaming bowl before they found seats and joined the others. They ate in silence, staring into the fire. Once Quinn had finished his meal, he cleared his throat and addressed them all.

"I know what we found today was a huge blow, but I think we need to put it aside and concentrate on coming up with a plan to free the town as soon as possible, before they kill anyone else."

Josh set his bowl on the ground beside his chair and his face had a hard set, "We need to kill them all!"

Cooper nodded and stood up, "I'm ready to go in and start picking them off!"

David frowned at the two boys, "Hey, I'm upset about what we saw today too, but we can't go looking for revenge! Acting in self-defence is one thing but we can't just go in and start murdering these men. That would make us as bad as they are!"

Josh and Cooper glared at David while Josh said forcefully through gritted teeth, "THEY DESERVE TO DIE!"

David held his hands up in a pleading gesture, "That's not for us to decide! We aren't the law. We don't get to play judge, jury and executioner!"

Alex's cold hard voice had all eyes swinging her way.

"That's where you're wrong. This isn't the old world. It's down to the basics now until some form of government comes forward. There are two sides, good and bad. They made their choice…they picked the wrong side! We will kill who we have to and turn the rest over to the townspeople once we free them." She looked around at the group and met each pair of eyes before continuing. "Tonight we make our plan and tomorrow we do it. I'm not waiting anymore. You can come with me or wait here. I don't care anymore what you choose. I've picked my side…it's time you picked yours!"

Her eyes held a fierce challenge and Josh and Cooper stepped towards her without hesitation.

"I'm in!"

"Let's do it!" he said as Quinn joined them with a nod. Dara and Lisa stood and agreed as well. Emily looked at David and went over and kneeled in front of him.

"David, they're starving, terrorizing and killing our families. We need to do this!"

He shook his head and rubbed at his face, "It's not that I don't want to stop them. It's…"

She cut him off by leaning away from him and standing. Looking down on him, she said, "I love you, David, but this is it. You need to decide now. Are you going to fight with us or not?"

His face drained of color and he looked at her like she had slapped him before searching the hard faces of his friends and finally nodding.

Emily gave him a tight smile and nodded before walking away to join the others. She knew he would do what was needed, but now she didn't know if they would be together after it was done. Suppressing the tears she felt pricking at the back of her eyes, she pushed those thoughts away for now. They were going to war.

They gathered around the picnic table and anchored the hand drawn map with two lanterns for light. Quinn had filled in the numbers of the guards at all the locations that they knew about and the total came to forty nine with sixteen unaccounted for.

Once everyone had studied the map he started to talk. "Okay, we can send a team over to the last roadblock that we didn't check today to confirm their numbers, but it's looking good that there will only be four based on the others we've seen. I like part of Alex's plan that she came up with but we will have to tweak a few things. Let me tell you all what I think we should do and then we'll toss it around and see if everyone agrees." When he got nods all around, he continued. "First of all, tomorrow night is when we go. She's right that we can't wait any longer. We leave the roadblocks alone and in place for the first part of the plan. We don't know when they rotate the guards and we don't want that to give us away too soon. We hit the farms first and we do it together. My place first because it's closest. We go in after dark and get the jump on the guards in the house. While most of us hold them, the others will go out and unlock the barn. We have a lot of extra guns that we can hand out to the people and *they* can decide what to do with the guards. Hopefully we can take them by surprise and we won't have to kill any of them, but we will do what we have to," he said this last part while looking at David, who nodded gratefully.

Quinn looked around at the others. "David's right in some ways. We can try to do this without killing all of them. Revenge might feel like the thing to do right now, but it's something that we will suffer from down the road. So, we will shoot if we have to, not because we want to." He looked at Josh and Cooper who had cooled down a little and they both gave grim nods in agreement.

"Alright, the next step is to explain the plan to the people we free on Grandpa's farm and convince them to go along with it. We will arm some of them to stay behind in the barn so they can deal with any new guards that are sent out. We can't have anyone running to town on a vendetta or the whole plan will fall apart. We hit each of the four farms like that and then split up and get into position at all four roadblocks. Once the sun is up and they send men out to check on why no one has come in from the farms for visiting day, we take out the roadblocks. We'll use the radios to stay in contact and with the extra men who will join us from the farms, we should have enough firepower to take them out and move into town."

Quinn paused to take a drink from his water bottle and then focused on Lisa. "I'm sorry, Lisa, but we will have to clear your house. It's on the outskirts of town and we can't have any guards that are there coming up behind us."

She looked at him with an empty expression. "Do what needs to be done. My mother picked the wrong side. It's on her head, not ours."

Quinn nodded and looked away quickly. The emptiness he saw in Lisa's eyes hurt his heart. Clearing his throat he continued with the plan.

"We will have to keep a careful count of how many guards leave town to go out to the farms. We want to have a solid number of who's left in town. Hopefully it will be less than ten at that point. Now this is the trickiest part. We know that ten of them usually watch over the women and kids at the school area but that could be changed when they send guys out to find out what's happening on the farms. We may have to make it up as we go when we see where the last guards are. The very last thing we want is for them to barricade themselves in with the women and kids as hostages." He looked around at the others and asked, "Any suggestions?"

Alex glanced at Emily, Dara and Lisa before sliding over to Quinn. Her face set in to stubborn lines when she answered him.

"Yes, but you guys aren't going to like it."

Josh looked up from the map and focused on Alex's face. What he saw there had his eyes widening and he started to shake his head.

"NO. No way! Whatever it is, Alex, no! I know you're the take charge, rush in and get it done girl but this is different! These guys are savage!"

She narrowed her eyes at him. "And what? We haven't faced savage more than once in the last month? We need to get this done! The only way to be sure that the women and kids get free is if we go in to that school. So here's my plan. You guys and the men who come with us surround the school and community center. You'll need to have people who can shoot a rifle well up on a few roofs for good coverage. Us girls go to the fence where Cooper and Dara made contact and slip in and blend with the prisoners. We will only be able to take handguns we can hide under our shirts but we will go in armed. Once the shooting starts outside, we take down anyone inside and lock it down until you give us the all clear. It's the only way we can control what happens in there."

Josh was sputtering and Dara laughed at him, "Forget it, Josh! It's a solid plan. I'm with Alex."

Emily didn't even look at David she just nodded. They all looked at Lisa expectantly and she just shrugged. "I'm good to go wherever you guys want me."

Alex frowned at her response. It was like Lisa had been scooped out and an automated shell was going through the motions. They would have to keep an eye on her and try to help her work through things once this was all over. She turned her head and met Quinn's eyes with raised eyebrows.

"Well?" she asked him.

His gaze was steady when he replied. "I flat out hate it and I'm scared out of my mind that I might lose you...but it's a go. It's our best chance, but you better be so careful, Alex...all of you have to make it out of there. We've come too far to lose any of you." His words might have been for all of them but his eyes never left hers and the love she saw in them took her breath away.

Looking in to his eyes at that moment, something clicked into place. It was an "oh, of course" moment for her and she finally saw her future was with Quinn. Tearing her eyes away from him she caught sight of Cooper. He was just turning away but she caught the look of loss on his face and felt sadness for him. He would have seen it on her face. Her choice had been made and it wasn't him.

Chapter Thirteen

They stayed up late in to the night going over the finer points of the plan before finally crashing and sleeping as late as possible. They would try and nap as much as they could the next day as they would be staying awake and running through most of the next night while they worked to free the farms. It was just past noon when Alex and Emily stumbled out of their bunks and joined the others for some food. Quinn, Josh and the other two boys had pulled all of the weapons they had accumulated out of the white cargo van and laid them out on the ground for an inventory. When Emily, David and Lisa got their first look at all the weapons and ammunition cases, they were speechless. After putting aside the eight assault rifles for the group's use, they were left with thirty five of the powerful weapons to hand out to the town's men. There were also various shotguns, hunting rifles and handguns they had picked up along their travels. They would be liberating the guard's weapons as well, so Quinn suggested that they hold back some of the assault rifles at camp in case something went wrong and they needed them in the future.

Once they had decided what they were taking to hand out to the freed men, they started to load the farm truck. The plan was to drive the truck and the three ATV's as close to Quinn's farm as they safely could before continuing on foot. When Quinn and Alex's farms had been secured, they would go get the vehicles and move them up closer before hitting Emily and Josh's properties. They would need them later in the plan to get in position to take out the roadblocks on all sides of town.

While the boys loaded the truck, Alex, Emily and Lisa made food. They used both ovens in the two campers to make batch after batch of buns that they mixed cut-up canned ham in, as well as huge batches of pancakes. They wanted to be able to give the freed men something to eat so they would have some strength to help attack the rest of the guards. It wasn't much, but it felt good to have something to feed the people they were going to rescue, and it kept them busy so they didn't dwell on what was coming that night.

Cooper and Dara had gone to scout out the final roadblock that was missed the day before. It was better to confirm the number of guards there instead of just assuming there were four.

Alex's head came up from the camp stove when she heard Dara call out. She and Cooper came into the campsite and went to the map to mark in the numbers before Dara walked over to Alex. Alex frowned when Cooper avoided looking her way and tried to think of what to say to him. Dara leaned over and took a deep smell of the browning pancakes before giving Alex a light hip bump. When she got no response from her friend, she followed Alex's line of sight until they rested on Cooper, who had dove into helping load the truck with the other boys.

"You're going to have to talk to him, Alex. Everyone saw the look between you and Quinn last night. It was obvious that you two are in love. Cooper's not in a very good place right now. He still blames himself for what happened to the town and now that he knows you've chosen Quinn, he's in a dark place," Dara told her with compassion.

Alex looked away from Cooper and flipped pancakes as she thought about what to say. She came up empty and huffed out a breath.

"What do I do? How do I explain to him that how I feel about Quinn just clicked in to place. I don't want to hurt him but I can't change how I feel!"

Dara rubbed her back in sympathy. "I know Alex, and the timing sucks, but you have to talk to him. Just be honest with him. Cooper's a really great guy and he will understand. But, Alex? You need to do it now, before we leave. We need his head in the game tonight."

Alex nodded and took a deep breath before handing the spatula to Dara and walking over to Cooper. He looked up at her as she came close and then quickly looked away and started to walk in a different direction.

"Cooper, please, can we talk?" she asked.

He came to a stop and she saw his shoulders slump from behind before he turned to face her. His eyes were filled with resignation as he looked at her. She waved her hand at the nearby trees.

"Let's take a walk?"

He only nodded and followed her on to a game path deeper into the forest. Once they were out of sight from the camp, she sat down on a fallen tree and patted the spot beside her, asking him to sit with her. He kept his hands in his pocket and his dark blue eyes were unreadable before finally sitting down with a sigh. Alex pulled a piece of long grass from the ground and fiddled with it as she tried to think of what to say. She gave up and dropped it to the ground before starting with the easier issue.

"Why do you keep blaming yourself for what happened to our town?"

His eyes showed surprise at the topic, as it wasn't what he thought she was going to say, and then he frowned and looked away without answering so she kept talking.

"Would you blame Dara for her mom being a drunk? Or Lisa? Her mother's ice-cold and working with the gang." When he only shook his head, she asked, "Then why do you blame yourself for your dad's actions? He made those choices, not you. You were thousands of miles away when it happened. How can you be to blame for any of it?"

Cooper scuffed his feet in the dirt and still didn't look at her when he replied. "In my head I agree with you but my heart feels guilty, like somehow I could have stopped him or made him a better person. I don't know...it's weird! I just can't stop feeling guilty. Besides, no matter what happens tonight and tomorrow no one in that town will ever forget who my father was and they will always blame me in some way." He finally turned and looked directly at her. His eyes were sad but resolved. "When this is all over, I'm going to have to leave. I can't stay here Alex. I'm sorry."

She scowled at him. "What are you talking about? You can't leave! Where would you go? Cooper, this is your home!"

He slowly shook his head and a small smile crossed his face at her outraged tone. "It's not. It's not my home anymore, Alex. You didn't hear the venom in that girl's voice when I told her my name. That's just a small sample of what it would be like living here."

Alex got up and paced around in frustration. She turned to him and threw her hands up.

"They will know that you're a hero! We'll tell them about how we made it across two countries and we wouldn't have been able to do that without you having our backs the whole way. We'll tell them how you fought to free them and their families! They'll know you're nothing like your father!"

Cooper had leaned back and was admiring her angry tirade. She was so pretty and full of life. His feelings for her surged and he forced himself to finish it.

"It's not only that, Alex. I'm in love with you and it would kill me to see you with Quinn every day."

Alex froze at his words and a soft "oh" escaped her as she felt her eyes prick with tears. She fought to find the words to explain.

"Cooper, I…it just, I didn't…Arggg!" She spun away from him and kicked at a tree in frustration at the hurt she could see in his eyes. She closed her eyes and took a deep breath before trying again.

"Quinn has been beside me since we were little. It feels like he's always been there and last night…I finally realized that he hasn't just been beside me, but inside of me too. My heart, he fills my heart. I'm so sorry."

Cooper leaned forward and picked an early spring daisy. He stood up and walked up to her and handed it to her.

"Never apologize for love, Alex. You and Quinn were made for each other. I'm happy for you. I mean it!" he said as she gave him a questioning look. "You guys are the best friends I've ever had. We're going to take back the town and kick some butt. We'll figure out the rest later, okay?"

Alex nodded and leaned in and kissed Cooper on the cheek. "Thanks for being such a great guy, Cooper. I'm so glad you left Disneyland with us."

Cooper smiled at her. "Me too. You should go on back. I just need a few minutes, okay?"

Alex nodded and held up the daisy and winked at him before turning and heading back to the campsite. Cooper sat back down on the fallen tree and watched her go. He was grateful for her support but he knew there was nothing left for him here. Once they had taken the town back, he knew he would slip away and try to find somewhere else he could call home.

When Alex walked back into the campsite, her eyes went to Quinn and she felt a quiver in her stomach at the look he gave her. She tore her eyes away from him and went to help the girls fill plastic bags with all the food they had made. She hoped there would be plenty of time in the coming days for her and Quinn to deal with the emotions they were feeling. Right now, though, they needed to focus on the plan.

They spent the rest of the afternoon trying to nap to get rested up for the night ahead. After a filling supper of stew and baked buns, they loaded the last supplies they were taking and headed out. Alex drove the farm truck with Lisa and Emily in the cab beside her. Cooper and Dara sat in the bed of the truck while Quinn, David and Josh followed behind on the ATVs. Alex kept the truck's speed down so the boys could keep up, and to keep the noise down. Her shoulders were tense and her hands sweated on the steering wheel. She was so worried that they would get caught at this crucial stage. Her shoulders relaxed with relief when they left pavement and headed down a dirt road to where they would leave the vehicles. When she came to the end of the road, she flipped the truck around so it was pointed back the way they had come and shut it off. She left the keys under the floor mat so they would be easy to find when they came back for the truck later that night.

They had given themselves plenty of time to get to Quinn's farm before dark. They would be carrying a lot of supplies through the trees and they wouldn't be able to move as fast as before. The boy's backpacks were filled with ammunition, and the girls had food and water. Everyone slung as many rifles as they could and they covered what they left behind in the truck with a tarp. Walking through the trees being so weighted down was a challenge, and it was slow going. They took breaks and after an hour they finally came to the clearing where their tree house was built. After a quick look to make sure it was clear, the group entered it and dumped the supplies against the trunk of the tree in relief.

Quinn, Alex and Josh left the others there and carried some of the supplies to the spot that she and Emily had used to spy on Quinn's farm when they had scouted it out. There was still an hour before the sun went down and they wanted to take a look at the farm before they lost the light.

Alex scaled the same tree and used the binoculars to scan the farm yard. There was no butchering going on this time and she could see men walking in from the far fields to the barnyard. They were setting up tables and Alex guessed that they were getting ready to feed the workers their nightly meal. There were only four guards in the yard that she could see, but the other two might be bringing people in from the fields. Alex tried to find Quinn's grandfather in the men crowding into the yard but he wasn't in sight. Her pulse went up when her mind flashed to the pit at the dump filled with elderly people. She silently prayed that the guards were smart enough to know the value of Harry Dennison's vast knowledge of farming. Her breath left her in a whoosh when she finally spotted him standing by a water trough that was being filled with water by a hand pump. She watched for a while, as men came up and scooped water out to wash off some of the dirt of the day before heading to the food line. When Harry turned his head in the direction of the trees, Alex felt like he was looking right at her. She knew that was impossible and the sun was going down behind her, with no tell-tale reflection coming from her glasses this time. A small smile crossed her face. Harry knew someone had been watching them a few days before and he was looking at the trees in hope that someone was coming to help them. She wished she could give him a signal but in a few hours it wouldn't matter. He would be free.

Alex swung her glasses away from the man and did another search for the two missing guards. When she saw them walking behind the last of the men coming in from the fields, she dropped the glasses back into her shirt and climbed back down the tree to Quinn and Josh. The smile must have still been on her face, because they gave her a weird look, so she told them what had happened the first time with the binoculars and how Harry had warned her with a hand gesture. Quinn just smiled but Josh started to laugh.

"I've got five bucks that says your grandpa doesn't even blink an eye when we open up that barn later. I've got another five that says he asks us what took so long!"

Alex snorted a laugh and threw her arm around Quinn. "Can't you just hear him? 'Did you bring me back a bottle of Crown from the duty free store at the border?'"

Quinn dropped a kiss on Alex's head. "God, I miss him. I can't wait for this to be over," he murmured against her hair.

Josh beamed at him like a proud father. "Look at you two! If this was high school, you'd be king and queen of the rebels!"

Alex rolled her eyes at him and pulled out the binoculars and offered them to Quinn. "Do you want to go up and take a look?" she asked, waving at the tree.

He flexed his healing leg and looked up into the branches before nodding. "It's been a while, but yeah, I think I can do it."

Josh gave him a disbelieving look. "Dude, if you fall out of that tree right before the big raid, you're going to be pissed!"

Quinn gave him a withering look and took the glasses from Alex. "At least I won't break half the branches on the way up and down, you lumbering fool!"

Josh lifted his nose in mock disdain. "What can I say? I make my presence known wherever I go," he said in a haughty, high class voice.

Quinn didn't respond but a smirk crossed his face as he turned and studied the lowest hanging branches. Josh gave a long suffering sigh as he came over and cupped his hands to give Quinn a lift up. Once he was over the first branch, Quinn quickly disappeared from view. Alex sat down next to the supplies and stifled a yawn. The waiting was draining and she just wanted to get moving with the plan. She pulled out some jerky and handed a piece to Josh. They worked on the meat for a while and Alex got tired of Josh shooting her looks so she asked him,

"What?"

He looked up in to the tree and not seeing Quinn, gave her a devilish grin. "About time!"

Alex shook her head and asked again, "What?"

"You and Quinn! It's about time. I've been waiting for you two to figure out you belong together for a few years now."

She raised her eyebrows at him. "Really, sort of like you and Dara? How long have you been sitting on those feelings? Hmmmm?" she asked sarcastically.

Josh ducked his head and his cheeks flushed red before he mumbled, "Just sayin!"

He was saved by the rustle of leaves above as Quinn made his way down the tree and joined them. Quinn had a light in his eyes that made Alex smile.

"Did you see your grandpa?" she asked him.

"Yup! He was getting a bowl of food and then he turned and looked right over here before going into the barn. He definitely thinks something's up. The guards put a beam across the doors of the barn once all the workers were inside. I counted six of them before they went into the house. Let's go get the others and get back here. I want us all to move forward to the tree line and watch for a bit before we lose all light. We need to make sure that they aren't doing patrols. When we hit them, it would be great if they were all in the house." He paused and bit his lip in thought. "Emily said Dr. Mack told you guys that there were some men on your farm that stayed in the house with the guards, right?"

Alex made a face in disgust. "Yeah, he said there were ten men that worked for the guards for extra food. Why? What did you see?"

He shook his head. "Nothing. The only people that went in the house were the six guards. I guess nobody here sold out."

Josh smirked. "More like, nobody wanted to cross your grandpa! Can you imagine having to face him every day if you picked the wrong side? That would just be stupid!"

Alex nodded her head in appreciation. "He's right, Quinn. Harry's probably the most respected man from here to Red Deer. No one would want to be on his bad side if they could help it."

Quinn laughed softly, "Grandpa might be old but he's definitely a force to be reckoned with. Anyway, that leaves us with just the six guards to take out. Josh, you and I will stay here and Alex can go back to get the others and then we'll get in place. We need a little light to see by to get ready so let's get going."

Alex swung her rifle on to her back and took off through the trees to get the rest of the group. She was happy to be moving and anxious to start the plan they had come up with. It was just the first step in freeing the town, but the next step was freeing her father.

She and the others made it back to Quinn and Josh just as the sun was setting. The forest was dim and getting darker by the minute. Quinn went over the first part of the plan one last time.

"Okay, it's almost go time guys, so pay attention. We will move to the tree line until we can see the house. It will be dark but there should be lights in the windows, either lanterns or candles so we will be able to see it. We stay still and watch for an hour to let them get settled in, then at my signal we move in. We use the barn, shed and anything else we come across as cover until we can get up beside the house. Leave the barn alone. Don't try and make contact at all. The last thing we want is to give ourselves away. We can deal with opening the barn after we have the guards secured. Once we get to the house, we need to be completely silent. We need try and find out where they are in the house, so I'm going to do some window peeking. Hopefully they will all be on the main floor and we can split in to two groups and come in from the front and back door. If any of them are upstairs we will have to split up even further and send some of us up. We won't know until I can get a look inside."

They would leave the extra rifles and backpacks at the base of the tree and just take what they needed to secure the guards. Once that was done some of them could come back and retrieve them to pass out to some of the men. They walked the forty feet to the tree line and spread out and crouched down. The yard was empty of people and all they could see was the dim outline of the outbuildings. There was faint light coming from around the curtains of the house but only on the main floor.

Once again, Alex fought a yawn. She was nervous about the mission and sitting and waiting was making it worse. Just like at her own farm the other night, the guards came out one by one and did their bathroom business. She felt Quinn stiffen every time the door to the house opened, spilling light into the yard. Alex kept her eyes on the second floor of the house for signs of light. She didn't want the group to split up any more than they had too. Ten minutes after the sixth guard had come out and gone back in, she nudged Quinn.

"We should go now before they go upstairs to sleep. It would be better if we caught them all on the main floor so we don't have to split up."

He swallowed hard before his face took on a grim expression and nodded. He turned to Josh who was beside him and murmured in a low voice that it was time to go. Josh turned to pass it on to Dara so Alex told Emily who passed it down the line in the other direction. When Quinn stood everyone else came to their feet and they moved out of the cover of the trees and into the yard. They made a diagonal line to the back of the barn and stayed in its deep shadows as they skirted around it and the house came in to view once again. In groups of two, they crossed the empty yard on silent feet until they were all pressed up against the side of the house. They stayed low under the few windows on this side and waited as Quinn crept around the house peeking in windows.

Alex could hear the faint noises of men talking but couldn't make out the words. A shiver ran down her back when a loud burst of laughter rang out. She turned her head and tried to make out the faces of her friends but they were only dark outlines. Quinn was only gone for a few minutes but it felt like hours to Alex, as nervous sweat started to coat her body. She was concentrating so hard on keeping her heartbeat down and staying calm that she flinched when Quinn tapped her on the arm.

He put his mouth against her ear and whispered, "They're all in the kitchen playing cards. I counted all six of them. We split up now. Our team takes the back door and Josh's team takes the front."

Alex nodded her understanding and he moved down the side of the house telling the others and then returned to Alex's side. They split apart and moved to the back and front of the house. Alex, Quinn, David and Emily were taking the back door and Josh, Dara, Cooper and Lisa went to the front.

Alex's group crouched at the back door that led directly in to the kitchen and paused. They wanted to give Josh's group time to get into place. When the walkie talkie clipped to Quinn's belt clicked twice he turned to the others and nodded. They had practised how to enter the house back at the campsite and they all took their positions. Quinn was on the left of the door and Alex was on the right. She would turn the knob and push the door open for Quinn who would enter first and move to his left with Alex coming in right behind him and moving to the right. Emily would follow and go left with David last. He would stand in front of the door. Four faint clicks happened at the same time as they slipped the safeties off their rifles. Alex was surprised to find her heart and hands steady as she reached over to turn the knob. A quick thought passed through her mind that she would be a quivering mess after this was over. She turned the knob and shoved the door hard.

Quinn was moving before she even had time to pull her arm back and she swung her body up from its crouch and followed him through the door. As soon as Quinn moved to the left, she brought her rifle up and stepped to the right. She saw Emily come in from her peripheral vision but her eyes were on the six guards. Five were seated around the kitchen table she had eaten at so many times and one was standing with a bowl in his hand at the counter, a spoon halfway to his gaping open mouth.

Quinn barked out a command, "Hands where we can see them!"

The split second of shock had frozen the guards, but it quickly wore off and Alex saw one of them reach for a handgun at his waist. Her eyes narrowed and she let out a warning.

"Touch it and you're dead!"

His hand froze for a split second and Alex saw the calculation in his eyes before he went for it. She didn't have time to squeeze the trigger of her gun before the man was blown backwards and a loud shot rang out in the room. Her eyes tracked over to where it had come from and she saw Josh standing in the doorway that led to the front of the house. He gave a curt nod and moved to his left so Dara and Cooper could enter the kitchen. Alex turned her eyes back on to the guards and without any feeling called out, "Next!"

The guards all looked at her and they must have saw something on her face that convinced them they would all die if they if they tried anything, because they all slowly lifted their hands.

Quinn shot a glance at Josh and Cooper. "We've got them covered. Start checking them for weapons."

They both slung their rifles over their backs and moved forwards to search each man. One of the guards had a permanent scowl on his face and when Josh patted him down for weapons he growled at them.

"Those people out there aren't going to thank you for this when our associates take their revenge out on their wives and children!"

Josh had taken a step back from the man but before he could respond, Quinn took two steps forward, reversed his rifle and slammed it into the scowling man's jaw. Josh smirked as the guy slithered to the floor unconscious. He spared a look at the other men.

"Anybody else got something they want to say?"

When they just stared back at him, he shrugged and checked the next man for weapons. Once the men had been searched, Josh and David left the kitchen and cleared the rest of the house to make sure it was empty. Josh came back with a roll of duct tape and started taping the unconscious man's arms and legs. The group of teens stood guard until the all the men were secured. Emily and David offered to stand guard over them while the rest of the group went out to open the barn and explain to the men inside what the plan was. Cooper stepped forward after studying David's pale sweaty face.

"I'll stay with Emily. I think David could use some fresh air."

When everyone looked at David, his face flushed and he looked away. Josh stepped up to him and squeezed his shoulder.

"Come on, man. Let's go give the good news to the people."

David shrugged Josh's hand off and walked out the back door. Josh stared after him sadly. He knew his friend was having a hard time with them killing people, but it was something he would have to get over. This was only the first step in the plan, and there would most likely be more killing before the night was over.

There were five lanterns in the room so Quinn and Dara grabbed two and with Alex, Josh and Lisa left the house and headed to the barn. They walked across the yard to the barn and Quinn handed the lantern to Alex. He went to the beam holding the door closed and paused. After a minute had passed, Alex set the lantern down on the ground and walked up to him and put her hand on his arm.

"Quinn?"

He kept his head down and his eyes on the beam.

"I...he...I'm not..." he trailed off, not finding the words he needed.

Alex knew what was going on in his head. She had felt the same way when she saw her father.

"It's okay, Quinn. He'll know you did what you had to do. He'll understand."

Quinn turned his head and met her eyes. His were full of gratitude that she understood what he was feeling and he gave a nod before lifting up the beam and stepping back. Josh and David garbed the handles on both doors and pulled them back leaving Quinn and Alex standing in the middle of the doorway. Alex lifted her lantern higher and the light shone on Harry Dennison's face. He was standing just inside the doorway like he had been waiting for them all along.

Chapter Fourteen

Harry Dennison's faded watery blue eyes locked on to his grandson. The years of hard living working the land showed in every line and fold on his face. They stood staring at each other as emotions fought across the older man's face. He finally took a step forward and reached out his work gnarled hands to grip Quinn's shoulders. His voice was gravelly and chocked full with emotions.

"I knew...I knew you would make it back. When I saw the flash in the trees a few days ago I hoped it was you. I heard a gunshot. Are you all okay?"

Quinn made a muffled noise that was half-sob as he nodded yes. Harry's face broke for a half second before he used his powerful hands to pull his only grandchild to him and wrapped him close against his chest. He closed his eyes and thanked the Lord for bringing the boy back to him. A sniff and whimper had his eyes opening and zeroing in on Alex who was watching the reunion with tears pouring down her face. One of his long arms let go of Quinn and he reached out and plucked a curl from her shoulder and he gave it a gentle yank before pulling her into his arms with Quinn.

"Red, I never doubted for a minute that you would get my boy home."

Alex let out a half laugh against his chest before pulling back and wiping her face of tears.

"What can I say? I must have been a sheepherding dog in a prior life, but it took all of us to get this far." She waved Josh, David and Dara forward.

Harry took in their faces and smiled and nodded at them all. He looked past them and when he didn't see anyone else, turned concerned eyes on Alex.

"Emily?"

Alex smiled. "In the house with Cooper, watching the guards."

Harry's face went hard and he took in the rifles they were all carrying. He cleared the emotion in his throat.

"Leave it to you bunch to get some new toys at the end of the world! I'm guessing you know what the situation is. It's not just our farm that's in trouble."

Quinn had finally found his voice and he peered deeper into the barn at the men who were staring back at them.

"We do know what's going on at the other farms and in town. We have a plan but if we want to be able to free everyone then we need to work together. If anyone goes running to town right now we will lose the chance to free everyone," he said the last part to the men who were moving closer to the group.

Harry nodded curtly and turned around to address the men he had been held captive with.

"Alright, I know everyone is worried about their families but my grandson is right. We can't go storming the town without a plan or they just might take it out on our loved ones. The first thing we need to do is…dispose of the men in my house. We can't take the chance of them getting away and alerting the rest of the gang."

He named five men who stepped forward and he had a quiet conversation with them before they left with Josh to deal with the guards.

Alex knew what he had meant when he said to dispose of them. Her hardened heart knew it was what needed to be done but she was glad it wasn't her that would have to do the killing. Her head came up with concern when she thought about the guards being shot, so she stepped over to Harry.

"They can't shoot them!" she blurted out.

Harry's brow sank in compassion. "I know it's hard to understand that we have to kill them Alex but…"

Alex was shaking her head and she cut him off. "No no, that's not what I mean! I agree they need to disappear, but the sound of a bunch of gunshots might carry over to my place and alert the guards there!"

His face changed to one of surprise. "I mentioned that to the men I sent in to the house. No one from your place will hear anything." He paused and studied her relieved face. "You understand why they have to go?"

A faint flush came up onto her face but she kept her eyes steady on his. "We didn't fly home, Mr. Dennison. We've had to fight our way through in some parts. We…had to…" she trailed off, not able to say the words to this man she admired and respected so much."

Harry turned his eyes onto Quinn, who was looking down at his feet and then to the other teenagers that had fought their way home. David looked like he was about to break out into tears. Harry saw what they had to do on each of their faces and took a ragged breath.

"It's alright, Alex, all of you. You did what you had to do to survive. As long as you fought on the side of good you did the right thing." He looked to each one of them and saw that David had begun to weep, so he strode over to the boy and laid an arm around him.

"You listen to me, all of you listen! I've lived longer than almost all of your years combined and this is what I know. The good Lord gave us the means to fight evil and he is only disappointed when we stand back and let bad triumph. The meek shall NOT inherit the earth! The strong and the right will! Let this weight on your shoulders go. You all fight for good and He is proud!"

The men that had been watching and listening since the barndoors opened came forward and reinforced Harry's words. There were pats on backs and hugs given. Kind words were spoken and thanks given for all that the teens had done. One by one, the teens that had fought so hard felt a weight lift from their hearts.

There wasn't enough room in the farmhouse for all the men while they went over the plan for the rest of the night's mission so they stayed in the barn with a few more lanterns to light it up. Emily, Alex, David and Cooper ran back into the trees to retrieve the supplies they had left there, and the girls were happy to pass out some of the buns they had made earlier in the day. Quinn unfolded the hand drawn map on a table they had taken from the house and explained the plan that they had come up with. He laid out all the locations of the guards and what they needed to do to keep the element of surprise. There were a few people that wanted to just take off towards town right away but they were quickly dissuaded by more level heads.

Once everyone had been briefed on the next step, ten men were picked for their hunting and firearms knowledge to go to Alex's farm with the teens. It was decided that Lisa, David and Emily along with three more men would walk back to the truck and ATVs and bring them forwards to Quinn's farm. As soon as Alex's farm was liberated, they would drive it over and hand out more guns and food. There was some grumbling about the kids continuing with the raids. Some of the men wanted them to stay back and let them take over, but they were soon silenced when the teens made it clear that they would be a part of rescuing their families or they would go it alone. After all they had done and how far they had come, there was no way they would not be included. After much arguing, it was finally agreed upon that the teens would stay out of the houses and open the barns once the guards had been neutralized.

Alex checked her watch and was surprised to find that a few hours had passed since they had first left the tree line and started the raid. She was anxious to get moving and see her father again. They had a lot to accomplish before the sun rose with three more farms to free and then get into position at the roadblocks. When everything was finalized and they were ready to move out, Alex gave Emily and Lisa a hug and they cautioned each other to be careful. The three teens and three men going for the vehicles would have to go on foot. If they took the guard's vehicle, they would have to travel on the road in between Quinn's and Alex's farm and there was too much chance of the guards at the next farm hearing it.

Ten men and five teens ghosted across the field and road that separated the two properties. Alex, Quinn, Josh, Dara and Cooper stood guard in the yard with their weapons ready as the ten men entered Alex's house. No light shone from the windows and Alex guessed that everyone inside was asleep. As she stared up at the house she wondered if the taint of these evil men would ever be erased from her home. Light flashed through a few of the upstairs windows with the sound of gunshots. Alex counted eight shots before silence came again. The sound of a window being shoved opened came to her ears and she moved around the house in the direction it came from.

Josh's voice had a hard tone to it as he yelled out, "On your knees, hands up!"

Alex skidded to a stop beside him and pointed her rifle at the dark shapes of people spilling out of the window. A lantern flared to life and Dara held it high so the light spilled on a jumbled pile of bodies trying to separate themselves under the open window. Alex was studying each man's face as they managed to remove themselves from the pile, and her confusion turned to cold anger when she remembered Dr. Mack telling her that these men had collaborated with the guards. Once they had all separated and gotten on their knees, one man called out to Josh.

"Is that Josh Green? It's me, Billy Stover, don't shoot! We've been held hostage by a horrible group of men and forced to work as slaves!"

Josh kept his eyes and rifle steady on the pleading man.

"I know who you are, Mr. Stover. I can honestly say I didn't much care for you before this all happened and I'm not really surprised you're in your current situation."

The man frowned at Josh, "Watch your tone there, young man! I'm a respected member of this community and you will talk to me with respect!" he proclaimed with indignation.

Josh let out a bark of laughter before he spoke coldly. "Do I look like I just fell out of the stupid tree? You sold any respect you might have deserved for a few extra bowls of food. It's not my place to judge what happens to you and your friends but there will be consequences for what you all did." A sneer crossed his normally good natured face. "Now shut your yap trap!"

The man whined and blubbered and tried to justify what he had done, but Josh just faked a yawn. Alex had to turn away to hide her smile. Josh always could make her laugh.

The men filed out of her house with grim expressions and the teens handed over their prisoners.

Alex didn't know what would happen to them and to be honest, she didn't really care. She only cared about one thing right now and it was opening the barn doors and seeing her father.

The people inside the barn had been alerted by the commotion in the yard and the gunfire from the house. When the beam was taken down, they were all on their feet staring at the doors. Alex didn't have to look far for her father. He was standing just inside the door with a panic-filled face that changed to relief when the first person he saw was his daughter. Alex's face broke into a huge smile as she rushed to him and the tension left her shoulders when she saw him standing on his own two feet. He limped towards her with his arms spread wide and caught her up in to a hug that only a father could give. He pushed her back to arm's length to get a good look at her.

"My pretty girl! I thought maybe I dreamed you had come. When I woke up the day after you snuck in it all felt like a dream."

Alex smiled and sniffed back her happy tears. "You had a pretty high fever, dad. I'm so glad you're better. I was so scared!"

Jonathan Andrews pulled his daughter close again and gave thanks she was safe. He saw Quinn and the others over her shoulder and sent them a smile of gratitude. Harry Dennison walked into view and came over to shake his hand. His deep gravelly voice was full of determination when he explained the situation and what had to be done. Dr. Mack had joined them and listened to the plan for the rest of the night and next day.

His voice was grim when he asked, "What happened to the guards?"

"They won't be needing your services, doc," Harry told him with a meaningful look.

Dr. Mack's shoulders slumped a little but he nodded. "I can't say I agree but it's probably for the best."

Harry took a good look around the barn and scanned the men who had been held captive.

"We need to round everyone up and let them know what's happening so we can get over to The Mather's farm and then the Green's. Let's get to work. There will be plenty of time to talk once we finish this."

Alex left them to go over the plan with the other men and headed back outside to talk to her friends. Josh had already alerted Emily that the farm was secured and she, David and Lisa where headed their way with the vehicles and extra supplies. Quinn rested his arm around her shoulder while they waited. Her heart was lighter after seeing her father safe and on the mend, but she knew they had a long way to go before the rest of their families were safe. A loud obnoxious voice rang out from the barn and she turned to look in the door. She didn't really need to see who it was to know that her old gym teacher, Mr. Beck, was squawking out his opinion. It did make her smile when she saw Quinn's grandfather place one of his big hands on the man's shoulder and squeeze in a not so friendly manner while talking to him. She turned away at the slightly pained expression on his face.

Josh was watching with an expression of glee and he snickered. "How many times have we all wanted to accidentally throw a dodge ball at that guy's head?"

It wasn't long before the truck and ATVs pulled down the drive and supplies were handed out. Twenty men were heading to Emily's farm and they planned on taking another ten from there to Josh's. His farm had the most guards and they wanted to have plenty of guns to take them down. A brief argument came when

Alex's father insisted that the teen's stay back but he caved in when they promised to not enter the house where the guards would be. They had come too far not to see this fight through.

Emily's farm was freed almost as easily as the first two had been with one exception. One of the guards had been outside relieving himself, but he quickly surrendered when he saw the wall of guns pointed at him. They kept him secured as they dealt with the remaining five guards in the house. None of them made it out.

Emily's reunion with her father brought tears to Alex's eyes and he was completely surprised to find his sweet daughter carrying such a big rifle. Once the townspeople had been briefed on what was happening, they all turned to the only guard left for information.

The man was a complete mess. He had tears and snot running down his face as he blubbered and pleaded for his life. Like the true coward that he was, he gave them all the information they asked for. Once the questions were answered, Harry unslung a rifle he had taken from one of the dead guards and used it to motion the man to his feet. When the sniveling guard realised what was about to happen he fell forward onto his stomach and begged.

"Please, please don't kill me! I swear I never hurt anyone! I just stood guard! Please…give me a trial, a lawyer, something?! This is murder!"

Alex was starting to agree with the man. There had been a lot of killing so far tonight and maybe this man should be treated differently. She looked around at the other faces staring at the man and saw there were others that felt the same. The decision was made when Josh took an angry step forward.

"You didn't hurt anyone? Really? How about the big hole we found in the dump? Know anything about that?"

The guards eyes flared wide and he slid his eyes away from Josh before answering.

"I don't know nothing about that!" He obviously was lying and Josh used his boot to prop him back up.

"You lying piece of filth! We scouted the whole town! We know everything you bastards have done! We know about your little pleasure house and what happens to the girls that work there! We saw the latest victim thrown on the pile of bodies in the dump!" Josh's face was bright red in fury and he was screaming so hard by the end he was spitting.

The terrified man fell back on his butt and tried to scoot away from Josh. "No, no that wasn't me! I've been here all week. I didn't have anything to do with that!" Something seemed to click behind the man's eyes and he looked at the faces around him. "You guys took out Jerry and his crew, didn't you?" When he was met with blank stares, he explained. "We sent out a crew to scavenge and last I heard they hadn't come back. We all just figured they had found a good stash and were partying it up somewhere, but it was you guys, wasn't it?"

While he was talking, Quinn was quietly explaining what they had found in the dump. Alex saw Harry's face go pale and the men around them that heard Quinn stepped back in shock. Fast movement caught her eye and she saw the anguished face of Mr. Beck as he snatched a rifle away from one of the men. He took two steps towards the guard on the ground and in one motion leveled the barrel and pulled the trigger. Two men were quick to disarm him and pull him away. Alex had to turn away from him when he started to sob that his mother had been at the nursing home.

The guard's body was dragged away and a crew volunteered to go in to the house and remove the bodies and clean it up. The team that was going to retake Josh's farm was assembled and ready to go.

Alex glanced at her watch and stifled a yawn when she saw it was after three in the morning. They only had a few more hours before they needed to be in position to take out the roadblocks. Alex looked around for her friends and saw Quinn and Josh talking quietly together. Dara and Lisa were leaning up against the barn and Alex thought that they looked like they were sleeping. Emily was still wrapped in her father's arms and Alex wondered if he would ever let his daughter go again. She scanned the yard and finally found David and Cooper standing off to the side. David was still looking shell-shocked and Cooper was staring off in to the night. Alex stared at Cooper sadly. She wished there could be a happy reunion for him as well. It wasn't fair that he had come so far and fought so hard with the rest of them, and yet he had no one waiting for him to come home.

Josh and Quinn approached her and broke her from her sad thoughts. Quinn studied her face.

"Are you okay?" he asked with concern.

"What? Oh yeah, I'm fine. I was just thinking it wasn't fair that Cooper has no family left. He looks so alone. I'm worried about him. He told me after we were done freeing the town, he was going to leave."

Josh looked over at Cooper in surprise.

"Where would he go?"

Alex just shook her head. Josh's face took on a stubborn expression.

"I'll talk to him. He's our family now and I'll make sure he knows it."

Quinn nodded and Alex sent them a grateful smile.

"So, are we about ready to go? All this standing around is making it hard to stay awake."

Quinn brushed her hair away from her forehead.

"Are you and the other girls still planning on going over the fence? We have a lot of men on our side now. We should be able to take whoever is left in town."

Alex started shaking her head. "We have to come too. If they barricade themselves in with the women and kids they might start shooting hostages. We need to have people inside in case that happens. We know what they're capable of. None of this will matter if we lose our moms."

Josh gave a curt nod. "We figured you'd say that so I want you to do us a favor. You and the other girls need to stay here and get a few hours of sleep. There are enough people going over to my place that you guys don't need to come. Besides, we won't be doing any of the heavy lifting anyway."

Alex looked over at Dara and Lisa who had slid down to the ground with their backs to the barn wall and heads resting against each other.

"Are you sure, Josh? We should finish this together."

"Really, Alex, it's okay. You guys get some rest. You'll need to be sharp for what's coming."

Quinn shoulder checked Josh lightly with a grin.

"He just doesn't want Dara to see his dad crying all over him. Right, Joshy?"

Josh tried to look mad but gave it up.

"What can I say? The Green men love large! We're not afraid to show our manly
      emotions."

Alex had to smile. Josh's dad was a big solid man with an even bigger heart. She had seen him tear up in pride over his kids many times. She thought he was a huge sweetheart.

"All right, if you're sure, we'll grab some sleep here but you better come back and get us!" she warned.

After they promised they would be back, they rounded up Cooper and David and left with the rest of the crew across the field to Josh's farm. Alex pulled her two sleepy friends up from the ground and she and Emily led them in to the house for some much needed rest.

Chapter Fifteen

Alex smothered a yawn as she peered through the blinds from an upstairs window in the house Cooper and Dara had used to scout the schools a few days before. She could see a few women and kids in the park walking down the cultivated rows that had been planted. She turned away and flopped down on to the bed beside Lisa. Dara was leaning against a wall flipping through an outdated magazine she had found, and Emily was pacing back and forth with nerves as they waited for Quinn to radio them with the news that the roadblocks had been taken out. It had been easy to sneak into town and make their way to this block of houses and all they were waiting for was the final number of guards still left in town. When no one showed up for visiting day, they expected the gang to send out a few men to check on the farms. Once that happened, the guards at the roadblocks would be taken out and Quinn would radio them before the freed and armed townspeople would move in.

Emily and Alex knew that their fathers would never agree to let them be a part of such a dangerous plan so they had lied to them and told them they were going to the campsite to bring back more supplies. Both girls felt incredibly guilty about lying to their fathers, but they refused to leave their mother's fates to chance.

Once again the waiting around for something to start was draining on them all. All of the girls wore baggy sweat shirts to conceal the handguns they were taking into the school. They had wire cutters to get through the fence and they were ready to go and finish this. All they needed now was the final number of guards they would have to face if they locked down the school.

Even though they were expecting it, they all flinched or jumped when the walkie talkie squawked and Quinn's voice came over it.

"This is Quinn. Are you there? Over."

Dara picked the radio up and responded for him to go ahead.

"Everything outside of town is now clear. They sent six more guards out to check on the farms. They were taken care of at Josh's place and we've cleared all four roadblocks. No injuries this time."

Alex let out a sigh of relief. While the girls had been sleeping, the raid at Josh's farm hadn't gone as smooth as the others. They had lost one man and another was injured when one of the gang members was alerted to them entering the house and a short but brutal firefight occurred. Alex was brought out of her thoughts when Quinn came back on the line.

"The total count we've come up with from the farms, roadblocks and the highway is fifty five dead. So there is still ten or less in the town somewhere. Over."

Alex knew that a lot of the guards had been killed last night but the number fifty-five seemed huge to her. She shook her head at the waste of life, so many dead on both sides. Was this what they had to look forward to for the rest of their lives? Would things ever get back to normal?

"We're moving into town from all sides and we should be in range of the school and community center within twenty five to thirty minutes. You girls should go now if you can."

Dara keyed the mike after getting nods from the others. "We're heading out now. Good luck, over."

Quinn's end came back with static before he said, "Be careful. Please, be careful, over."

Dara went to clip the radio to her belt when a new voice came over the radio. It was loud and it was mad.

"Alexandra April Andrews, this is your father! You better not be planning anything! I heard what Quinn just said and it better not have been for you girls!"

Alex's eyes flew wide and she threw a hand up to her mouth. Before she could even reply, another voice came over the radio.

"Emily Mather, you get your butt back home right this minute! You girls need to leave this to the men! You're all too young to be playing war!"

Emily's face went from little girl guilty to stone cold mad in a split second. She snatched the radio from Dara.

"Dad, I know you think I'm just a little girl but I'm not. We haven't been "playing" war. For the last six weeks we've been living war! We know what we're doing. I love you and I'll see you after this is over. Now please stay off the line. We need it clear for the next part of the plan. OVER!"

She turned and thrust the radio at Alex with a challenging stare. Alex squeezed her eyes tight in dread and blindly held out her hand for the radio. Emily slapped it in her palm and she brought it to her mouth.

"This is Alex. Sorry, dad. I love you. Over."

The room was silent as they waited to hear any response. A few heart beats later, it came.

"My baby girl, be so careful. I just got you back!"

Alex swiped her eyes of tears before responding.

"I'll bring back mom, dad. Love you, over." She clicked the button back to transmit a second later. "Quinn, we're going now, over."

"Copy that, good luck!" he responded right back.

No one moved or spoke for a minute until Dara broke the mood.

"You guys are soooo grounded!"

After a beat of silence they all broke into tension-relieving laughter. Lisa stood up and adjusted her sweater to cover her gun. In a perfectly deadpan tone she said, "You should offer to give up your iPhone."

Dara chimed in, "Or your computer. No internet for a month!"

Alex faked a heart-broken expression.

"Damn, I really wanted my cell and the computer for paper weights."

Emily was shaking her head.

"You just watch. I bet they try and take away our guns!"

The other three girls shot her panicked looks until Alex broke out into a devilish grin.

"That's okay. We left a bunch back at the camp site. I know a great place to hide them!"

The girls might have been making light of the situation, but as they filed out of the room and down the stairs they were all conscious of just how dangerous things were about to get for them.

The wire cutter made quick work of cutting a section of fence big enough for them to slip through and Dara left the tool in the grass as they split apart and started to pretend to pick weeds from different rows. Dara and Cooper had told them what they had seen when they scouted the park, so they all had garbage bags that they stuffed grass and a few plants in to make it look like they were working like the other captives. The girls moved from row to row and slowly got closer to some of the other women in the field. When Alex and the others were only one row away from two women on their knees pulling weeds, they looked up and noticed the four new arrivals. The first woman was in her forties and with her was a girl around twelve. The older woman stared at them in confusion and opened her mouth to speak but Emily, who was closest, gave a sharp shake of her head. They had only seen one guard walking the field, but now that they were closer to the building they could see three more milling around the tables set up on the concrete that skirted the high school.

Alex had made her way closer to Emily and the woman and girl. She was about to ask the woman about the number of guards when the sound of gunshots came from the distance. Everyone froze in place for a split second before all their heads turned in the direction that the shots had come from. A shout had them looking back the other way. The guard who had been in the field was running towards them, waving them towards the building. The girls stayed on their knees as he got closer and the woman and girl seemed to cower against the ground.

"Get up, you lazy bitches! Get in that school right now!"

He bellowed angrily at them. He passed Lisa and Dara and stopped a few feet from the group of four.

"I said, get in the school. NOW!"

His face was angry but Alex could also see a flicker of fear pass through his eyes before they went wide in shock. Lisa had stood up when he passed her. She came up beside him and stuck the barrel of her gun into his armpit when he raised his arm to point at the school. She didn't even hesitate when she pulled the trigger. The guard staggered sideways and flopped to the ground. They all heard the shot, but it wasn't as loud as it should have been because the barrel had been pressed against his body.

Alex and Emily looked towards the school in panic, afraid the guards there would be running towards them but they were surrounded by all the women and kids they were trying to herd into the school and not one of them turned in their direction. Alex let out a breath of relief and turned back to her group.

"We're good. They didn't hear it. Throw your garbage bags on top of him and let's go!"

The woman and girl were staring with big eyes at Lisa in shock. Emily had to shake the woman's arm to get her to refocus.

"Hey, snap out of it!" When her eyes came to rest on Emily, she explained,

"The men at the farms are free. That's them doing the shooting out there. We need to know how many guards are here at the school."

"They're free? My husband and son? They were at..."

Emily cut her off. "Lady, we need to move! How many guards?"

It was the young girl that answered her. "There were six when we started work this morning." She shot a glance at Lisa. "There's five now, I guess. I don't know where the rest are."

Emily nodded and sent the girl a quick smile. "Good, okay, we need to move. You two head to the back of the park to the fence. There's a spot that has been cut. Go through it and find a house to hide in. Don't come out until the shooting stops for at least an hour. GO!"

The girl flashed a fast look back at the school before yanking on the woman's arm and pulling her away deeper in to the field. Alex, Emily, Dara and Lisa, who had hidden her gun again moved quickly towards the school. They saw the last group of captives disappear through the door and only one guard left standing outside. He turned from the door and scanned the yard before catching sight of the four of them. His face was filled with a scowl and he used his shotgun to motion them forward before scanning the field behind them for anyone else.

There was only the five of them left outside the building that Dara could see, and the door to the school was closed. She barely whispered "I've got this one" to the others. As Alex and Emily passed the guard, Dara who was next in line, pretended to stumble and just like Lisa had, brought the gun she had hidden behind her back around and pressed it hard against the guard's chest before firing. It would have worked perfectly except that he had his finger on the trigger of the shotgun that he was pointing in the air and he spasmed and pulled the trigger. The sound of the shot was huge and the girls looked in horror at each other as the guard lay dead at their feet.

Alex broke first and grabbed Dara, "Doesn't matter! There's four left. Hide your gun, Dara. We go through the door looking scared and panicked. Cry if you can!" She turned to Emily who had her hand on the door and nodded.

Emily pulled the door open and they all put on scared expressions. They ran inside and had only gone five feet before another guard rounded a corner and aimed a rifle at them. All the girls dropped to the floor and held their hands up. Their terrified expressions made the guard discount them as threats and he re-aimed this rifle at the door they had just come through while yelling at them.

"What happened? Where's Johnny? I heard his shotgun go off!"

Alex took the lead and said in a pitiful voice,

"I don't know! He was holding the door open for us and he shot at something in the field. We just dove in and the door slammed behind us."

She put enough whine in her voice that the guard shoved her out of the way in disgust and headed to the outside door. Alex spun away on her knees and took a quick look down the hall for more guards. When she saw it was empty she spun back around and pulled her gun from under her sweater. She steadied her breathing and lined up her shot. The bullet went straight to its mark through the guards back and destroyed his heart, killing him instantly.

As soon as he fell, Dara, Emily and Lisa were on their feet and pulling Alex up. She stuffed her gun back into her waist band and they pelted down the hallway. When they got to the corner they slid to a stop and peeked around it both ways. There was no one in sight but they could hear people crying and making noise to the left.

They pulled back from the corner and Emily looked at the others.

"They're in the gym."

Dara nodded. "Makes sense, there's no windows in there so it's a good place to lock them down in. Three guards left if no one else came. What do we do now?"

Lisa shrugged. "We go to the gym."

Alex shook her head.

"They're going to notice us just strolling in through the main doors. Not only that, our moms are in there. As soon as they see us, they'll give us away. They won't be able to help it. They think we're in California!"

"Okay, so we don't go in those doors. We use the girl's locker room to go through to the gym. The door from there leads to the small hallway where the equipment room is. We stay low and just slip around the corner and into the crowd. It sounds pretty noisy in there so if anyone we know spots us we just try and shut them up fast."

The girls looked at each other in consideration before Alex finally shrugged.

"Okay, I got nothing else so let's go for it. Flying by the seat of our pants seems to be working so far!"

Dara snorted, "Yeah, as long as we don't get shot in those pants in the next few minutes!" Her face turned thoughtful. "The last three guards are not all going to be in the gym. They'll have at least one or two guys at the front of the school keeping watch. Should we split up?"

Lisa started nodding.

"I should go in the gym. We know my mother isn't in there to give me away," she said with a trace of bitterness.

Emily gave Lisa's arm a pat. "I'll go too. Dara, your Mom and brother are both in there so you have a bigger chance of being recognized. Alex, out of all of us, you're the best shot so if you can take them out from a distance, do it. Lisa and I should be able to get close to whoever is in the gym with all those people as cover."

They were all in agreement, so after quick hugs they split up. Emily and Lisa went left towards the girl's locker room door and Dara and Alex went right, farther into the school as they made their way towards the front entrance. Alex found it surreal to walk through the halls of her high school with a loaded gun hidden under her shirt. It made her so mad that buildings like this that was supposed to shelter and care for students had been turned into a prison. She only hoped that one day it would go back to what it was intended for.

Cursing from the front of the building had the girls slowing down and moving even more cautiously. They heard a deep hard voice bark out an order.

"God damn it, I can't see anything from here! Go check the south side and see if you can find where that shootings coming from!"

A second voice chimed in, "You got it, boss! Do you think it has anything to do with the guys not coming in with the workers this morning?"

The first voice was harsh and aggravated when it replied.

"What do **you** think, dumb ass! Of course it does! If there's shooting in town that probably means the farms and road blocks aren't under our control anymore! We need to keep those women and kids locked down to use as hostages. After you look on the south side, go check on Johnny and the other guys and make sure they have everyone in the gym."

Alex pointed down the hall to the south to Dara and the girl nodded and took off as quietly as she could. They now knew where the last two guards were and Dara could surprise the one leaving the front of the school. Alex flattened herself inside a doorway to a classroom as seconds later one of the guards came down the hall and walked towards where Dara had just run to. Once he was past and had turned a corner she sneaked out and quietly moved towards the front entrance where they had heard the two guards talking. She was halfway there when she heard hard footsteps heading in her direction. She swore at herself for not having her gun out and ready as she threw herself into another doorway and crouched down with her head tucked down. There was no way the guy wouldn't see her so she went with the scared victim routine and hoped she would get a chance to surprise him. Alex knew the only reason any of this had worked so far was because these jerks underestimated a bunch of teenage girls and saw them only as hostages. She also knew that their luck couldn't last forever and prayed that it wouldn't run out in the next few minutes.

"What the hell! What are you doing out here? GET UP!" were the words yelled at her, followed by a big boot kicking her in the leg.

Tears of pain welled up in her eyes from the kick and they helped with her cover story when she whimpered,

"Please don't hurt me! I didn't know what to do!"

Alex looked up at a very tall man with a shaved head and the coldest grey eyes she had ever seen. His face was blank with indifference as he stared at her and she felt her skin crawl. There was nothing human in his look.

"Get up and get to the gym."

He reached down and hauled her up and off her feet with one hand and Alex was shaken by his strength. He started to turn away from her with his big hand still clutching her arm when the sound of two gunshots rang out from the back of the school. They were closely followed by another shot from down the hallway where Dara and the other guard had gone.

Boss's face was still indifferent when he turned back and dragged Alex towards the front entrance. He spoke calmly and almost to himself.

"Change of plans. Looks like the party's over in this town." He gave her arm a brutal yank as she tried to slow them down and sent her a dark look.

"Move it, girl! You're my ticket out of here."

When they got to the front doors of the school, he pulled Alex in front of him and wrapped one of his big arms around her upper chest to use her as a shield. He scanned the parking lot and road for movement before pushing the door open and stepping out with Alex in front of him. They made it down the big front steps and into the parking lot before men started popping up from behind cars and in between houses across the street. They were all pointing guns at them.

Alex could barely breathe from how tight the man was holding her and she pawed at her sweater to reach the gun she had in her waistband. The Boss had a shotgun in his free hand but all he could do was point it at the men standing in front of him because of the way he was holding Alex. When he bellowed at them to back off, she finally caught the hem of her shirt and got it raised enough to get a grip on the handle of the gun and out of her pants. That's when time seemed to slow down.

Just as Alex pulled her gun and pointed it down and back at Boss's leg, Cooper broke from behind a parked car and ran towards them, yelling her name. He had his assault rifle up and was looking for a shot when she pulled the trigger. Her bullet hit Boss in the knee and the arm around her throat let go and flew wide. Alex dropped to the ground and rolled away from the raging man who brought up his shotgun and fired. At the same time he fired, almost every man facing him pulled their triggers and Boss was hit by at least eight bullets, killing him where he stood.

Alex didn't see him die. Her eyes were glued to the sweet boy with the bad reputation who had just been shot in the chest. Their eyes held each other and she saw love and regret and pain in his before he crumpled to the ground.

Chapter Sixteen

Time sped up. Alex launched herself to her feet and sprinted towards Cooper's fallen body. She fell to her knees and was stripping her sweater off in seconds. Her chest was heaving with sobs and she was chanting the word "No" over and over again as she balled up the sweater and pushed it hard against his chest. Alex fought the person who pulled her away but went limp when she saw Dr. Mack take her place. He had a duffle bag that he was pulling supplies from and his hands were a blur as he fought to keep the precious blood from leaving the boy's body and save Cooper's life. She was being held from behind, much like Boss had held her as a shield but there was no threat in the hold, only comfort. She realised that it was Josh holding her when she heard him curse under his breath.

Alex tore her eyes away from Cooper and the doctor when she heard her name being called frantically. Her gaze swept past Quinn and David and she saw her father limping towards them with a panic-filled face. When he spotted her, his face changed to one of relief. Before he could come any closer the front doors of the school were thrown open and a huge flood of women and children came pouring out. Alex saw families come together with tears and laughter. She knew she should be happy about the town being free but found herself looking away and back down to Cooper. Dr. Mack had covered his chest in gauze pads and was wrapping it in place. He leaned back and looked around the crowd.

"I need to get this boy to my office! I need a stretcher!" he yelled out to be heard over the noise of the happy crowd.

"MEDIC! We need a medic here!" rang out and had everyone turning to find the source of the voice.

Josh's arm dropped away from Alex and the curse he let out was full of bitterness.

"Son of a bitch!"

He stalked to the soldier that had called for a medic and started screaming in his face.

"WHERE WERE YOU? Why weren't you here before? Cooper...my friend...where were you!"

More soldiers were walking up behind the first one and military trucks were turning onto the street a few blocks away. One of the soldiers raised his weapon and pointed it at Josh, barking for him to step back but the one who had called for a medic raised his hand to stop them. The soldier didn't know what had happened here, but he could see the anguish on this young man's face. It was a look he had seen again and again as their relief convoy had moved through town after town since the pulse had knocked the power out. He put his hand on Josh's shoulder and squeezed it in comfort.

"I'm sorry. We tried to come as soon as we could. We have surgeons who can try and help your friend."

The anger drained from Josh's face and he started to cry. He was shaking his head as he turned and walked back to his friends with tears pouring down his face. Alex opened her arms to him as he mumbled,

"It's too late. You're too late."

Alex knew he wasn't just talking about Cooper. He was talking about what they had been forced to do to free their town. It was something that they would have to carry with them forever.

Dara, Emily and Lisa made their way through the crowd and joined them. There was nothing any of the teens could do as soldiers ran up with a stretcher and carried Cooper away with Dr. Mack hot on their heels. Alex watched them go and shook her head at the irony of the Canadian Army showing up after a bunch of kids had done most the fighting. She just prayed that their presence meant that Cooper would be okay and their town could get back to some semblance of normal.

A small body came barreling through the crowd and threw itself at Dara. Her little brother Jake almost took her off her feet as he wrapped his skinny little arms around her. The look of love and relief that crossed Dara's face was heartwarming and she just closed her eyes and raised her face to the sun. Josh had gotten control of his emotions and joined the pair. Jake beamed a smile his way.

"Josh! Your mom and sister are so cool! They've been taking care of me!" He turned back to Dara and his smile dimmed. "I don't know where mom is. She never came to stay with us and the bad guys."

Dara cupped her worried little brother's face.

"Don't worry about that right now. We'll find out where she is later."

She shot a look over his head at Josh and he nodded and turned to scan the people around them. He didn't have to look very far to see his dad, mom, and sister, Sofia, in a group hug. His trademark grin flashed across his face for a split second before he teared up again and joined them for his own family reunion.

Quinn was surrounded by his grandparents, and Anna Dennison kept reaching out to touch him, running her hand through his hair and then grasping his hands.

Alex saw Emily with her parents and she had Lisa with her. She smiled when she saw Emily's mom pull Lisa into a loving hug. She searched the crowd for her own family, and found her mother sobbing into her dad's chest. Alex threaded her way past David and his mom and little sister who were crying and smiling and holding each other in a tight little huddle. Alex's dad saw her coming over her mom's head and the love on his face helped to fill some of the emptiness she was feeling inside after seeing Cooper shot. When he turned Alice Andrews around so she would see her daughter, her breath caught on a gasp and she lunged at Alex.

"My baby girl! My brave, beautiful girl! You're here, you're safe. Oh Alex...I was so scared I had lost you!" she said in a voice choked with emotion as she held her tight.

When her dad wrapped his arms around both of them, Alex closed her eyes and let the weight of the last six weeks go. For that moment, she let herself be a little girl safe in her parents' arms again.

** ** ** ** ** ** ** ** ** **

Two days had passed as the town and its people tried to put the pieces back together. Families were reunited and loved ones lost were mourned. There were meetings held and new leaders were nominated as they tried to put together a plan to survive in this new, powerless world. The soldiers gave them news of what was happening in other places. There were many decimated cities and towns and a lot of people had died but they also brought news of communities coming together trying to rebuild. In Alberta, the pulse had stopped a hundred kilometers north of Edmonton. The small population to the north had taken in refugees and was working around the clock to send working parts south. It would take decades to fix and replace all that had been lost to the pulse and the world would never be the same.

Almost everyone in the town had gathered to see the soldiers off. They were moving on to other areas to check for survivors and give aid, but they had given the town a working radio and the frequencies to the base the army had set up between Red Deer and Edmonton. The soldiers had also spent the last two days recruiting any able body person willing to join them. They needed more people to work at trying to restore order to the province. No one was surprised to hear that the western and northern parts of the country had fared better than the east. They had been in contact with other units across Canada that had specialized communications equipment that had survived the pulse. The lower population base and existing farms of the prairies had gone a long way to keeping people alive. Hundreds of thousands of refugees had fled north and west from the huge cities in lower Ontario and Quebec and the army had set up a huge base in Thunder Bay to process them and send them further west. The logistics of feeding so many people were huge but the massive acres of farmland in the prairies would need the labour of so many to plant and harvest future crops.

There had been limited contact with the United States, but what they had heard was similar. Cities emptied and people died on the road. Smaller population centers fared better and areas with strong leadership had started to rebuild. The criminal element did its worst to the population but with the old laws no longer functioning, justice was swift, often brutal, and most times, final. No longer would criminals have more rights than their victims, and if lawyers were not quite outlawed, they were strongly frowned upon if they tried the old way of delays and technicalities for their clients. The world no longer had the time or the patience for long drawn-out trials and appeals when just providing the basics of survival already exceeded resources at hand.

Generations of people who were used to instant gratification had to learn a new way of life.

Entertainment, when there was time, stopped being about overpaid athletes, pop stars and movie stars. No one cared what the latest reality show star was wearing anymore. Local dances and bands filled that void, with card game parties and pot lucks replacing restaurants and movie nights. For many towns, market day was looked forward to. People came together to barter or trade what they had and it replaced hours of mindless spending at shopping malls. One of the biggest changes for many people was that they now actually got to know their neighbours instead of just waving as they drove by. Life was much simpler, but it was hard. Medicines ran out and food was scarce until it could be harvested. People died and people lived and it would never be the same.

Alex stood with Dr. Mack a few feet away from her family and friends. They watched as soldiers loaded Cooper into the back of one of the trucks on a stretcher. He was going to recover, thanks to the quick work of the army surgeon and a few blood transfusions, but it would take a long time. When he had regained consciousness and was told what had happened he had asked to go with the soldiers and be a recruit once he had healed. The army was taking quite a few people with them back to their base before continuing on their aid mission, and nothing the teens said could change Cooper's mind. He didn't have any family left in the town and felt he would always bear some of the blame for what his father had done.

Dr. Mack surveyed the crowds lining the street like they were waiting for a parade and sighed. Alex looked up at him, her eyebrows raised in question.

The doctor looked around them before saying quietly, "This is going to sound terrible but that gang saved a lot of lives." At Alex's horrified expression he held up his hand. "What they did to the people of this town was horrible and in a lot of cases, evil. But they also made everyone work and they took all the food from every house and store and rationed it out. If they hadn't taken over, I have my doubts the town council could have gotten everyone to work together like that. There is a huge amount of food planted right now that will feed us this fall and winter. Without that gang, I don't know if that would have happened. People would have hoarded what they could until it was gone and then there would have been stealing and fighting among neighbours for any scrap they could find. Now we still have food in storage and crops in the ground. Look at all of these people, Alex. Most of them are in the best shape of their lives from the work they were forced to do. So many people in this town were overweight and unhealthy. They needed all kinds of medications because of that, but now they don't. I'm not saying it was a good thing and if it had of continued, people would have started to starve from the low rations, but a lot of people will live longer because of what they did here."

Alex looked away from the doctor with a frown and studied the people lined up on the sidewalks. There were some that were too skinny and gaunt but the majority looked healthy and strong. Their faces were tanned from being outside and she couldn't see anyone with a belly hanging over their belt. They did look good. She would like to think that her town and neighbours would have come together on their own but a small part of her knew that the doctor was right.

Alex was distracted from her thoughts as a woman walked towards her and her group from the army truck. She was completely out of place with her stylish hair and beautiful clothes. The woman's high heels snapped against the pavement as she glided towards them. Looking at the beautiful woman, Alex thought she could have come from the pages of a magazine, not the world of the past six weeks. As stunning as she looked, Alex noticed that there was no depth in her eyes as she stepped past Alex without a glance.

"There you are, Lisa. I wasn't sure if you would still be in the area."

Alex had turned to watch the woman and saw Lisa looking at her with no emotion. Alex realized that this woman was Lisa's mother.

"I wanted to let you know that I will be traveling with these soldiers back to the base. I'm told they have some electricity there and I would be more comfortable."

When Lisa didn't answer but just stared at her mother like she was a stranger, the woman nodded.

"Well then. Take care, dear."

She turned away and took two steps before stopping. Alex could see her face and the expression that crossed it was like something had just occurred to her. She turned back to Lisa.

"You could come with me."

There was no pleading or love in the statement. It was an afterthought.

Lisa cocked her head to the side and looked her mother up and down and her voice was filled with disdain when she answered.

"I'm sorry, Claire, but I'm not interested in being a whore. Besides, my family is right here and I couldn't leave them."

Lisa used the woman's name instead of the title of mother which she no longer deserved. Claire Kelly lifted her nose in the air and rolled her eyes just like her daughter used to do, before turning on her heel and walking back to her future customers.

Alex looked at her friends standing in a group. Quinn sent her a smile full of love, Josh winked at her and put David in a loose headlock, Dara shook her head at his antics and laughed. Emily had an arm around Lisa's waist and their heads leaning against each other's in support. Alex started nodding her head. They had come so far together and she realized that home might be defined by a place, but it was being surrounded by the people you loved the most that made it HOME.

The End